CAUGHT

Carter turned to see several shadows closing in. He bent his knees and put his hands up, ready to tackle his way out of this if he had to. But before any of the others could get there, a vine loop dropped into his field of vision. He noticed it at the same moment it slipped around his head.

Carter reached up to snatch the vine off, too late. It already had him, and pulled up tight under his chin.

Someone dropped from a branch overhead. The slack in the vine went even tighter, and nearly yanked Carter off his feet. Whoever it was hit the ground behind him and snaked both arms around his shoulders. The loop tightened again, cutting into his windpipe.

"*Stranded* is non-stop adventure!
If your kids love *Survivor*, they'll love this book!"
—Mark Burnett, Executive Producer of *Survivor*

READ THE ENTIRE SERIES!

STRANDED

BOOK 6

SHADOW ISLAND
DESPERATE MEASURES

JEFF PROBST

and CHRIS TEBBETTS

PUFFIN BOOKS

PUFFIN BOOKS
An imprint of Penguin Random House LLC
375 Hudson Street
New York, New York 10014

First published in the United States of America by Puffin Books,
an imprint of Penguin Random House LLC, 2016

CIP Data is available

Puffin Books ISBN: 978-0-14-751390-8

Printed in the United States of America

1 3 5 7 9 10 8 6 4 2

As we conclude another great Stranded adventure it brings me back to how it all began. Lisa, my brilliant wife, had the original idea and we centered it around our kids Michael and Ava—who give me the greatest gift every day when they call me dad.

Then we took their favorite cousins, Alyssa and Evan and Amanda and Abby and used their best qualities to create the other two characters. We had our family!

I've had so much fun hearing from all of you who enjoy the books. Your comments and in many cases your ideas have really helped shape the series.

Remember, the adventure you're ready for is the one you get! Go for it!   —JP

For Margaret and Paul, with love   —CT

CHAPTER 1

Carter pinwheeled his arms, trying to hold on to thin air as he fell.

It couldn't be done. In a second, he'd landed hard on a wide net of woven vines. The breath rushed out of him. He rolled twice, coming to a stop on his stomach.

Already, his right arm and leg had slipped through holes in the mesh. It left him bound up in the crisscross of vines as the net shook from the impact of his fall.

And where was Chizo? The other boy had dropped this way only a few seconds before. He had to be nearby—

The answer came right away. Even as Carter lay

tangled facedown, Chizo sprang into view. He leaped up from the ground, maybe six feet below. The net still separated them, but its gaps were more than wide enough to get an arm through.

Chizo's eyes were wild. He looked insane as he held the net with one hand and reached with the other. His fingers closed around Carter's arm and he dropped back to the ground.

Rough mesh scraped across Carter's face. Experience had shown him how strong these vines were. They were going to cut him to pieces before they'd ever break. And Chizo wasn't letting go.

"GET AWAY FROM ME!" Carter screamed.

He swung with his free arm. The punch he wanted to land only grazed off Chizo's shoulder. Chizo had gravity on his side, with both feet on the ground now, while Carter stayed tangled in the woven vines.

This was it. This was the moment they'd been moving toward since the first day of *Raku Nau*. The competition may have been over, but the two of them still had a score to settle.

Carter bent his left knee. It bought him enough

leverage to pull his other leg free and reel back several inches, but no more. Chizo wasn't giving up, either. He sprang off the ground a second time just as Carter pushed toward him again.

With a sickening smack, their foreheads collided in the middle. Carter heard a crunch somewhere inside his skull and fell back again.

His vision blurred. The world spun.

And everything went black.

CHAPTER 2

Jane stood on the beach, staring at the ocean. She clung to Vanessa and Buzz, watching for any sign of their brother.

Carter had to be coming, didn't he? He *had to*. And yet . . .

She couldn't even finish the thought. She knew better. *Raku Nau* was a competition for sixteen *seccu*. All sixteen of those winners' necklaces had been claimed. Jane could see across the bay to the top of Cloud Ridge where the *seccu* had been hung. Each of them had leaped for their own necklace, down through a misty void, and into the water. From there, it had been one last exhausting swim from the base of Cloud Ridge to the beach on the eastern shore.

Now, the vine that had once held the *seccu* was empty. Their friend Mima had been wearing the last one as she swam ashore moments ago. And Carter was nowhere to be seen.

"Carter? Carter?" Jane asked her, knowing the answer.

"Fah," Mima answered. It meant *no* in the Nukula language. Carter wasn't coming.

Jane looked at Vanessa on her left, then Buzz on her right. "What's going to happen to us?" she asked.

Neither of them answered. There was nothing to say, because there was no way to know. Carter could have been hurt, or worse. And without him, none of them were going anywhere.

Mima took Jane by the arm, pulling her away from the water's edge.

"Jane, Buzz, Ba-nessa!" Mima said. *"Ekka-ka, ekka-ka!"*

This way, she was saying, urging them off the beach. A *Raku Nau* finishers' celebration would be getting under way soon. The drumming in the woods had already changed, from an earnest, steady beat to something more joyful and expressive.

But how could they celebrate anything now? Turning away from the water felt like turning away from Carter. Jane dropped to her knees instead, sinking in the wet sand where the Pacific Ocean lapped at the shore.

The need had been for all four siblings—Jane, Vanessa, Buzz, and Carter—to finish the *Raku Nau* competition together. It was the only way to reach the remote island's eastern shore, where the tides were gentle enough to ride away from this place.

Shadow Island. That was Jane's name for it. The Nukula who lived here were masterful at keeping themselves hidden in the jungle's shadows, away from the outside world. They weren't bad people. Just the opposite. But the Nukula were also protective of their way of life.

Even if Carter had made it this far, the four siblings still would have needed some way of getting out to sea under the watchful eyes of the tribe. Then, and only then, could they hope to be spotted by a ship or a rescue plane.

But none of that mattered now. Without Carter, they couldn't even think about leaving. The four of them had been stranded here as a family, and they were going to leave as a family or not at all.

So was that it, then? Was Shadow Island their new home? Did this mean they'd never get to see Mom and Dad again?

No, Jane thought. *No. No.* That couldn't be the case. It just couldn't.

Or maybe that was what anyone thought when things went too wrong to imagine. Maybe it really was over and they just hadn't figured it out yet.

Buzz knew he had to be strong—stronger than any eleven-year-old should have to be. It wasn't fair, but that was beside the point. He could see Jane was losing hope. It showed in his little sister's eyes.

He'd been there himself. They all had at one time or another. Even Vanessa—who was the oldest, at thirteen, and always knew what to say—seemed out of answers.

"Let's get into the woods, you guys," Buzz said. "We'll figure something out. We can't do anything from here."

Mima had given up trying to coax them over. Already, she was halfway to the clearing, where the celebration would take place. They were all expected to gather there, away from the shore. The Nukula never lingered for long where they could be spotted by a passing plane or ship, and Mima had to answer to the tribe like anyone else.

"Buzz is right," Vanessa said. "We should get over there with the others."

"Why?" Jane blurted. "It doesn't matter what we do anymore. It was all for nothing!"

"You don't know that!" Buzz shouted back.

The force of his own voice surprised him. Then again, he'd never thought in a million years he'd have the guts to finish something as hard as *Raku Nau*. Images of the last three days flashed through his mind.

The Nukula village on the far side of the island.

The endless miles of mosquito-infested jungle.

The enormous obstacle course where they'd last seen Carter.

It was all supposed to bring them here to the eastern shore, and ultimately back out to sea, where Mom and Dad would be looking for them.

But Carter was still on Cloud Ridge, just short of the *Raku Nau* finish line.

And the clock was ticking. Nukula tradition held that all those who finished *Raku Nau* spend the night in celebration. Then, at sunrise, everyone would leave for the main village on the island's western shore. The tides on that side had washed Buzz and his siblings onto the island, but going the other way was potentially fatal. Without knowing any better, they had tried to paddle away from the western shore on the first day and had nearly drowned.

Not only that, but Mima's parents had lost their lives navigating those same tides several years ago, leaving Mima an orphan long before Buzz's family ever set foot here.

The only real option now was to leave from this side of the island, or not at all. Once they set out for the west, they wouldn't be coming back. Then it would really be over.

But it wasn't over yet.

Buzz knelt down and took the purple stone of Jane's *seccu* between his fingers. "Do you see this?" he said. "We earned these. That means something."

"It doesn't mean anything if Carter's not here," Jane answered. "What if we can't ever leave? What if we're here forever?"

The questions terrified him. Still, Buzz kept a stony expression on his face. The important thing was to get off the beach. As long as they were stuck here, they needed to live the Nukula way, by Nukula rules.

"Come on," he said. "We're going. Now."

"But . . . *Carter*," Jane said, pointing across the bay toward Cloud Ridge. "He's still back there with Chizo."

Buzz hooked a hand under his sister's arm and brought her to her feet. There was no knowing what to expect next, or what Chizo might do to their brother.

Still, they couldn't let any of that stop them. Not after everything they'd been through. If the last few weeks had taught Buzz anything, it was that survival meant putting one foot in front of the other—even when he was so scared he could barely breathe.

Like right now.

CHAPTER 3

Carter's vision swam as he came to. He was lying on his back on the net. When he reached up to touch his throbbing forehead, a golf ball–sized lump blazed with pain. His stomach clenched, but there was nothing down there to throw up. None of the *Raku Nau* runners had eaten in more than twenty-four hours.

He rolled over and looked down. Chizo sat slumped on the ground, hands around his knees, head bowed, and barely stirring.

Carter dragged himself to the edge of the net. He rolled off and dropped, ignoring the shock to his legs as he hit the ground. The pain was everywhere, but it couldn't be helped. This wasn't over, and his best bet now was to strike first.

It was impossible to know how old Chizo was, maybe thirteen or fourteen. Definitely older than eleven-year-old Carter. But that didn't matter here. On this playing field, they were equals.

Carter lasered his focus on Chizo. He pushed his feet into the dirt. And he charged.

Chizo looked up just as Carter hit him in a low tackle. It knocked Chizo flat. With a quick scramble, Carter was on top. The adrenaline rushed through him. He pinned Chizo's arms with a knee on either side. He pressed his left hand into Chizo's chest and cocked his right fist, ready to swing—

But then he stopped cold.

The dead look in Chizo's eyes was unlike anything Carter had seen before. Chizo wasn't even trying to fight back. He'd barely moved at all. And it wasn't just from exhaustion.

It was defeat. Carter had seen that look plenty of times back home, usually on the ball field. You could always tell when the members of the other team knew they were done. The fight drained right out of their eyes, leaving them blank and empty. Just the way Chizo's looked now.

It felt like staring into a mirror. Carter had everything he needed to win this fight, but something had just changed.

It hit him with a wave of clarity. *Raku Nau* was over. There was no winning anymore. They'd both lost. Carter wasn't going home, and without a *seccu* around his neck, Chizo's chance of becoming chief of the Nukula had just evaporated.

Other runners from the competition had begun to come off the course, too. They gathered around and seemed to be waiting for the next move. At home, there would have been a lot of shouting—*fight, fight, fight, fight.* But none of them said a word.

Carter stood up in a daze. When he reached out to help Chizo off the ground, Chizo smacked his hand away.

"Sorry," Carter mumbled. He got it. Even now, Chizo needed to save face. And there was no reason not to let him. Whether that made Carter a wimp or a bigger man in these people's eyes, it was impossible to say. The Nukula had their own way of thinking about things.

Out of the silence, an adult voice sounded. Carter looked up. One of the tribe elders stood at the top of the gorge that enclosed the giant three-level obstacle course around them. Her face was familiar. She'd been one of three adults acting as observers during *Raku Nau*.

A moment later, the woman stepped off the gorge's edge and onto the course. She walked across a section of vine mesh as if it were solid ground, then jumped and snatched a rope on the fly to slide down one level. There, she landed on a small platform only long enough to turn and free-fall to the net below. With a final, fluid move, she landed on her back, flipped over, and let herself the rest of the way down. The Nukula seemed as comfortable off the ground as on it.

"Ekka!" the woman said. She pointed west, where the gorge opened to the valley below. Immediately, all of the others started lining up. It seemed they were being told to head home—down from the peaks of

Cloud Ridge, into the jungle, and toward the Nukula village on the far side of the island.

Carter's pulse spiked.

What have I done?

The thought burned into his brain. Jane, Vanessa, and Buzz were waiting for him on the east shore. They'd be out of their minds by now, wondering what was up.

Losing *Raku Nau* had never even been an option. And yet, here Carter was. He'd never considered a scenario where he'd have to choose between his family's fate and someone else's. But that was exactly how it had gone down. In the heat of the moment, he'd sacrificed himself to allow Mima through.

Back home, he was always the competitive one. Maybe even the selfish one. But he'd changed. There was no denying it now. The only thing he could have done differently was to leave Mima behind and take the final *seccu* for himself. That was never going to happen.

The four of them owed her everything. If it wasn't for Mima, they wouldn't have made it past the first day. And the *seccu* was at least as important for her as it was for them. Today, Mima's new life in the tribe could begin. No matter what else went down, Carter knew he'd always be proud of the choice he'd made to help her.

But could Jane, Buzz, and Vanessa understand all that? And, maybe more important—could they ever forgive him?

Vanessa held Jane's hand as they headed across the beach toward the woods. Feast preparations were under way. The smell of roasting meat filled the air and made her stomach rumble.

Still, it was impossible to think about anything but Carter. As they got near the clearing, Vanessa took one last, hopeful glance over her shoulder. And out there on the water, something caught her eye.

"Wait!" she said.

It was Ani, paddling an outrigger canoe toward the shore. His long, thin frame was unmistakable, even from a distance.

"Ani!" Jane called out, and ran back toward the

water. Vanessa and Buzz were right behind her.

If they couldn't be with their brother right now, Ani was the next best thing. He knew what it was to be an outsider. He'd washed ashore on Shadow Island over a decade ago. He also spoke English. From the moment Vanessa and her siblings had landed here, Ani had done what he could for them while still keeping his loyalty to the Nukula. When they'd tried to leave from the western shore that very first day, it was Ani who stepped in to warn them, and to save them.

Ani had also been there on Cloud Ridge at the end of *Raku Nau*. He'd watched as each of them grabbed a *seccu*, took a leap off the ridge, and began the final swim across the bay to the eastern shore. That meant he'd know what had happened to Carter.

"Ani!" Vanessa yelled. "Over here!"

Ani turned south then, and began paddling his outrigger parallel to the beach instead of toward it.

"What's he doing?" Buzz asked. "Ani! Come back!"

He seemed to be headed for the island's easternmost tip, a hundred yards or more down the shore. There was nothing but jungle that way. The only true landmark was an enormous palm tree that grew way out over the water.

In fact, Vanessa realized, it was the biggest palm she'd ever seen. It dwarfed the other trees around it. A broad crown of fronds at the top shaded the shore from a hundred feet or more above the ground.

"Ani!" Jane yelled next. "Please! We have to talk to you!"

He looked over now and cocked his chin in the direction he was traveling. If they wanted to hear about Carter, their only choice was to follow along the beach. Several others had taken notice of Ani's arrival, too, and began heading through the woods in the same direction. Some traveled on the ground; others went from tree to tree, in the Nukula manner.

Vanessa, Buzz, and Jane took off running down the shore at the same time. As they headed toward the enormous tree, Vanessa heard someone shout out in a long, birdlike trill. The voice seemed to come from everywhere and nowhere at the same time, filling the air around them.

"Look!" Buzz said. He was pointing at the jungle

itself, near the huge palm. The foliage there had begun to shake. And then, incredibly, it all started to move.

Vanessa kept up her pace, squinting to make sense of what she saw. The wall of green at the base of the palm was slowly sliding away, like some kind of giant screen door.

Which was exactly what it was, she realized.

This was the genius of the Nukula. They used camouflage in ways unlike anything she'd ever seen. In the village, a man-made ceiling of bamboo and greenery shadowed the tribe from passing planes. Here, the screen hid an entrance for canoes. It ran across a swift-moving channel that flowed out of the jungle and into the ocean. Ani had already turned that way and had begun to paddle inland.

As they reached the channel, another call sounded out and the screen reversed direction. They were close enough now to see several young Nukula pushing it back into place. The screen was made from bamboo and natural foliage. The huge frame of it spanned the channel, coming to a rest against the giant palm's trunk on one side and another large tree on the other.

From the ocean, all anyone on a passing ship would see was a small river flowing out of dense jungle.

"That . . . is . . . *amazing*," Buzz said, speaking for all of them.

But there was no time to stand around gawking. "Come on," Vanessa said. "The sooner we get to Ani, the sooner we can get some answers."

They cut into the woods next, skirting the edge of the screen to head upstream after their friend. Their path took them right under the enormous palm. The inland side of the tree's trunk was strung with a square lattice of vines, like a rope ladder. It was more camouflage, Vanessa saw, barely even visible from up close. The ladder rose all the way to the top, where a small hut was tucked under the palm's enormous crown of fronds.

It was a guard station, Vanessa realized. That's where the voice had come from. It was all making sense now. This was the island's most vulnerable spot. Ani had told them as much, before *Raku Nau* started.

A small number of Nukula lived on this side of the island, protecting it for exactly the reason she and her siblings had been trying to get here. The most guarded place on the island was the only one that offered them any chance at all for escape. The odds were crazy. It was almost too much to think about.

Almost, but not quite.

Jane moved as fast as she could along the channel's muddy bank. It was hard to be patient, picking her way over the roots and rocks, but the woods were too thick for running, and the channel's current was too fast for swimming. It would only wash them back toward the ocean if they tried.

She could see Ani now, a hundred feet inland, tethering his canoe to a tree on the left bank. Several other canoes were already moored there, and a low thatched hut sat nearby.

Dozens of Nukula had already arrived at the same spot, including Mima. When she saw Jane, Buzz, and Vanessa coming, a rare smile lit up her face.

Jane pushed through the crowd, but before any of them could reach Ani, an unfamiliar boy stepped in her way. A girl about the same age stood with him. Both wore fierce expressions.

These were the eastern-shore guards, Jane realized. Both of them were barely older than the oldest *Raku Nau* runner. And neither wore the *seccu*. That meant they'd failed to complete *Raku Nau* when they had the chance.

"Um-sha! Um-sha!" the boy said, waving them back.

"We just want to talk to Ani—" Vanessa tried.

"Um-sha!" the girl repeated, waving a sharpened stick in their faces.

Mima was there now, too. She laid a hand on Jane's shoulder. It seemed to say, *Don't push it.*

Soon, a man strode through the crowd toward the front, while everyone else made way. Jane recognized the shape of the man's face and the heavy brows over his dark, staring eyes. They were the same as Chizo's.

This was Chizo's father, the chief of the Nukula tribe. He was the one they called Laki.

Back in the village, Laki dressed no differently than the others. Today, he wore a long cape made from overlapping leaves and strings of small shells. The leaves themselves had been coated in the three ceremonial colors of *Raku Nau*, like shingles of red, black, and white. On his head, he wore a band made from some kind of leather, with long narrow feathers hanging off the back.

"He's got to be wondering what happened to Chizo," Buzz said.

"I think everyone's wondering that," Jane said.

Chizo had been a favorite to finish *Raku Nau*. The entire tribe had expected him to be chief one day. But now, of course, that could never be. He would forever belong to the group of Nukula who failed to earn a *seccu*.

Ani stayed calm, answering Laki's questions without any emotion in his voice. Before long, Laki turned and called out to the two guards nearest Jane.

"Tinata eh fasto Chizo!" he said. *"Sha-hia!"*

Without a pause, both guards ran down the bank. At the water's edge, they dove, side by side, into the channel, where the current carried them off. Within seconds they'd reached the mouth of the channel, swum under the green screen, and disappeared toward the ocean on the other side.

"They're going to get Chizo," Jane said. "Aren't they?"

"I bet you're right," Buzz said.

"But . . . why?" Jane asked.

"I have no idea," Vanessa said.

"Maybe being chief's son means you get an automatic *seccu*," Buzz said bitterly.

"Maybe," Jane said, but the dark look on Laki's face told her otherwise.

Without another word, Laki strode back up the bank and into the lone hut next to the channel. Most Nukula dwellings were built into the trees, but not this one. It sat directly on the ground.

As Jane watched, Laki bent down and lifted up a section of the hut's bamboo floor. The section was big enough to block her view through the door, but it soon dropped back into place. And when it did, Laki was gone.

"Did he just go *down*?" Buzz asked.

"There must be a cellar," Vanessa said.

"Or a tunnel," Jane said. It was hard to put anything past the Nukula. They were incredible engineers. The question was, where would that tunnel lead?

"Ani!" Vanessa shouted out.

All the others except for Mima had begun to leave. Jane pushed through the departing crowd with Vanessa and Buzz to reach Ani on the nearly deserted bank.

"Where's Carter?" Vanessa asked.

"What happened to him?" Jane asked. "Is he okay?"

"He will be fine," Ani said. He pointed for them to follow the rest of the tribe. A trail cut through the woods here, and everyone was headed back toward the main clearing.

"What do you mean—fine?" Jane said, trying not to shout. "Ani! What happened?"

"I will explain what I can," he told them. "But come. It is crucial that you stay with the tribe. Now, more than ever."

Buzz walked double time along the trail to keep up with Ani's long stride. He peered left and right, into

27

the dense greenery around them, as they went. It was amazing how fast the jungle could swallow you up, like some kind of living beast. A few quick steps off the path were all it would take.

"Ani, can you tell us?" Vanessa repeated from behind. "What happened to Carter?"

"And what happens now?" Buzz asked.

Ani answered without slowing. "Your brother stopped Chizo from completing the course," he said. "And he allowed Mima to finish ahead of him."

Mima turned at the sound of her own name. She seemed to sense what they were talking about. It looked as though she wanted to cry but didn't know how.

"Now Laki has sent for his son," Ani continued. "Chizo's conflict with your brother has cost the tribe a future chief. The leadership will pass to someone else. And Chizo will be exiled to *Trehila*."

"*Trehila?*" Jane asked.

Ani pointed back in the direction of the giant palm. "It is the outermost guard post for the island," he said.

"And what happens to Carter now? And to all of us?" Vanessa asked.

"You will be welcome in the village, but Carter's life will not be as easy. He will share a hut with the *otana*—those who do not finish *Raku Nau*. Without the *seccu*, his role in the tribe will be that of helper, and worker," Ani told them.

Buzz felt the tears on his cheeks before he knew he was crying. It was all coming so fast.

"That isn't fair!" he said. "We're supposed to stick together!"

"What you know as fair and unfair is different here. There is no dishonor in being *otana*. All roles are important to the Nukula," Ani said. "But you will not see Carter again until you return to the village. Your best choice now is to become members of this tribe, as I once did."

The idea of it took Buzz's breath away. He stopped with his hands on his knees.

"Buzz?" Jane asked.

"Ani?" someone called from ahead. *"Ekka-ka?"*

When Buzz looked up, one of the women at the back of the crowd was staring at them. They were lagging behind, and the other Nukula seemed to have noticed.

"*Ah-ka-ah*," Ani called back with a wave. Then he continued on the trail and gestured for Vanessa, Buzz, Jane, and Mima to follow.

"What do we do?" Jane asked.

"I don't think we have a choice," Vanessa said. "We stick with the tribe. At least, until we see Carter again."

Buzz nodded and took a deep breath. "Vanessa's right. We have to find him before we can do anything else. But then we'll figure something out," he said quietly. "With or without Ani's help."

CHAPTER 4

Soon, they came to the main clearing. People were preparing food and cracking coconuts around the fire, where a skewered boar steamed and spat juices into the flames. A small circle of drummers provided a constant, jangling beat that filled the air.

Bum-bum, bum-bum-ba-DUM-bum . . .

Bum-bum, bum-bum-ba-DUM-bum . . .

For Jane, it all felt strangely familiar—the sense of celebration, the smell of the food, and, most of all, the drums. That thumping rhythm carried her mind back to a day not so long ago, even if it felt like forever. It was the day they'd all become one family: Mom and Dad's wedding.

Just three months earlier, Jane and Carter's mother had married Buzz and Vanessa's father in a small ceremony in the backyard of the new house in Evanston. Everyone had been given a job. For Jane, it was carrying the rings up the aisle, where they all stood together until the last "I do."

After the ceremony, a band played into the night. It was good music, fun music. The percussionist had even let Jane sit in and pound away on the bongos for a couple of songs.

Bum-bum, bum-bum-ba-DUM-bum . . .
Bum-bum, bum-bum-ba-DUM-bum . . .

Looking back, it was strange to think about the nightmare that lay ahead of them that day. There was the shipwreck on Uncle Dexter's boat. The thirteen days of surviving on Nowhere Island. And then their near-rescue, when Mom and Dad found them with the help of a private search operation.

They'd been *so close* to going home again. But then one rogue current was all it had taken to snatch that chance away. The four kids had been swept out to sea in their life raft, faster than anyone ever would have imagined. The night they spent tossing over the waves before landing on Shadow Island had been as endless as any Jane could remember.

Now here they were, fighting to get back out to sea again. The idea of returning to the open ocean was terrifying, but it was also their best chance of rescue. The only thing scarier was thinking about never seeing Mom and Dad again.

Bum-bum, bum-bum-ba-DUM-bum . . .

Bum-bum, bum-bum-ba-DUM-bum—

"Jane?" Vanessa called. "Keep up!"

Jane blinked out of her waking dream. Vanessa was waiting for her, and watching with tired eyes. Her sister seemed just as exhausted as Jane felt. But what did it matter? Buzz was right. There was no changing what had happened, and no use looking back. The only useful thoughts now were about putting one foot in front of the other.

"I'm coming," she said.

From the main clearing, Ani led them up a second

trail, away from the celebration. All of the other *Raku Nau* winners and their families were already heading that way.

Before long, another hut loomed into view. The trail ended at its doorway, where two more guards were stationed. The hut itself was far too small to hold everyone who had already come this way, Jane noticed. And that could only mean one thing.

Sure enough, as they stepped inside, Jane saw a square hole in the bamboo floor where a trapdoor had been raised. Beneath it, a ladder descended into a dark hole. The line of people ahead of them had already started down. A flickering light from someone's torch showed dirt walls and timber supports below the floor, but nothing else.

"Where are we going?" Vanessa asked.

"To the marking ceremony," Ani told them. "It is the last act of those who run *Raku Nau*. You should prepare yourselves."

"Prepare how?" Buzz asked.

"With strong minds," Ani said, and tapped his fists in the Nukula manner.

Jane had learned the gesture from Mima, and returned it to Ani. She curved her fingers into fists, turned her knuckles inward, and knocked them together with a double tap. As far as she could tell, it meant *be strong*.

And so she would. They all would. Not that they had much choice.

Vanessa led the way down the ladder ahead of Buzz and Jane.

The air cooled as she came into a crowded, low-ceilinged tunnel. The earthen walls were supported with raw timber, and the tunnel itself smelled like dirt. Straight ahead, a torch in one of the elders' hands showed some kind of wooden door. Behind them, in the other direction, there was nothing but darkness.

"Where does that go?" she asked, but nobody answered.

"Ani?" Jane said.

"I'm here," he said from somewhere in the dark.

With that, the door swung open, wider and higher

than Vanessa ever would have guessed. Soft daylight spilled into the tunnel from the room beyond.

They moved with the group into a large round chamber. Laki and two elders were already inside, tending three large stone pots over a fire in the middle of the room.

Vanessa took in as many details as she could. The ceiling was domed, made from another lattice of foliage-covered bamboo. It bulged into the jungle itself, like a fifty-foot-wide skylight, overgrown with leaves and vines that hung down nearly to the floor.

There were three other tunnels, too. It seemed clear that Laki had come from the one on the right. It pointed back in the direction of the canoes and *Trehila*. The other two openings went to the west and north. It all laid out in Vanessa's mind like a half-finished map.

While Laki supervised, the elders used long sticks to lift the steaming pots off the flame and set them onto the dirt. Next to that, a stack of woven-frond mats sat with a pile of thin, stringy vines.

Everyone seemed to know what to do. All of the other *seccu* winners moved in single file around the circular room to form a wide ring. *Raku Nau* had begun with a fire circle. Now it would end with one, too.

Slowly, the adult family members stepped into the circle and turned to face their own loved ones. Ani, who had been speaking with Laki, now came to do the same.

As he faced Vanessa, Jane, Buzz, and Mima, a lump rose up Vanessa's throat. Ani wasn't their father, and Mima wasn't their sister, but they were as close to family as it was possible to have found in this short, bizarre time on Shadow Island.

"Thank you," she whispered to Ani. Mima squinted at her, and seemed confused by the emotion.

"Hold up the hand you used to claim the *seccu* on Cloud Ridge," Ani said, and then repeated it in Nukula for Mima. Vanessa and Buzz raised their right hands; Jane raised her left. And Mima had already bent down to pick up one of the frond mats.

"Now face me," Ani told Vanessa. "You first."

The other adults were using the vines to tie screens around their own children's arms. Jane knelt down to help Mima while Ani began to do the same for Vanessa.

"What are we doing, exactly?" Vanessa asked.

"You will choose a color," Ani said, and indicated the still-bubbling pots. Each one held a different liquid— deep black, bloodred, and milky white. They were the colors of *Raku Nau*. "Then you will place your *seccu* arm into the dye," he continued. "Red signifies fire. Black signifies earth. White signifies the trees. All of these give life to the Nukula."

Vanessa stared at the steaming liquids. The vine-and-frond wrapping pinched her skin as Ani knotted it down, but that was the least of her worries. It was hard to concentrate.

"Red," Buzz answered. "For fire."

Jane nodded in agreement. Fire it was. They would all do the same.

Already, several others had dunked their wrapped arms into one pot or another. Their faces were fixed, but not calm. Two of them, a boy and a girl, stood gritting their teeth, up to their armpits in the hot red dye.

Vanessa held a shaking fist over the red pot and tried to clear her mind. It was the same feeling as watching a dark storm roll in across the Pacific. There was no avoiding this now, only getting through it.

With a fast move, she plunged her whole arm into the cauldron. The liquid was hotter than any shower she'd ever taken, and she shuddered from the pain. Everything inside her said *pull back*. But with Laki and the others observing, she didn't dare.

The vinegary smell of the dye made her eyes water, too. She blinked several times, fighting off the dizziness, and locked her knees to keep from stumbling over.

"How long should I do this?" she asked.

"As long as you can," Ani answered, while he tied on Buzz's mat. "In the eyes of the Nukula, you are now adults. The choice is yours."

Vanessa took a breath and let it out. How many times had she wanted to be treated like an adult back home? More than she could remember. But that was no comfort at all right now. The only thing that mattered was gutting through this and putting it behind them.

For Buzz's sake. For Jane's.

And for Carter's.

Carter was the first to hear the messengers as they

approached. He'd been following at the back of the line of *Raku Nau* losers, out of the gorge, down from Cloud Ridge, and into the jungle heading west. The sound of the drums from the eastern shore had begun to fade behind them.

But now—a voice.

"Betta! Eh Laki, betta!"

He turned around to see two young Nukula, dripping wet and running toward them. Their faces were unfamiliar.

"Hey!" Carter called out to the front of the line. "Hold up!"

A few people turned around. The elder who had brought them this far barked out an order, bringing the line to a stop. Then she doubled back to greet the incoming strangers.

After a short conversation, the elder turned and called out to the group again.

"Chizo!" she said. *"Ekka-ko!"*

Ko? In the Nukula language, *ko* was used to address an enemy. That much Carter knew from his time on the island. Something very strange was going on, but what? Why would Chizo be an enemy to the tribe?

Still, Chizo didn't pause. He jogged right past Carter to where the messengers were waiting. A moment later, the group of three turned and headed uphill, back toward Cloud Ridge.

Everyone else broke from the line then, following after Chizo and calling out. Only Carter stayed put.

Before Chizo disappeared around a bend in the trail, he stopped and turned back, long enough to knock his knuckles together as the Nukula often did. The others all returned the gesture.

And as they did, Chizo looked straight at Carter, across the fifty yards of ground between them.

Carter's nerves went electric. It was force of habit. Chizo had tried to destroy Carter's chances in *Raku Nau* from the start. But there was no hatred in his eyes now. All Chizo did was raise his chin as if he were saying good-bye. Or maybe to indicate something behind Carter.

When Carter turned to look, there was nothing to see but empty jungle. What was that about?

And then he realized. Or at least, he had an idea.

Chizo was showing him a way to escape, wasn't he? Everyone else was still half a football field away. Even the elder had turned her back for the moment.

Was it some kind of trick? Or was Chizo paying Carter back for the mercy he'd shown on the floor of the gorge? Carter could have easily won that fight, but instead, he'd stepped off.

Now, his mind was spinning with new possibilities. The fastest way to reach Buzz, Jane, and Vanessa on the eastern shore was to head up and over Cloud Ridge. That was the way Chizo and the messengers would go.

But it couldn't be the only way, Carter thought. This was an island, after all. What would happen if he headed *around* Cloud Ridge to the north? Worst-case scenario, he'd hit the ocean and use the shoreline to guide him east, toward the sound of the drums.

He had to try, anyway. Any second, the others would turn back and the chance would be gone. That meant he had to disappear. And he had to do it right now.

Without another thought, Carter sprinted into the jungle.

CHAPTER 5

Carter pushed deeper into the woods. The trees were close, but the ground was free of brush. It gave him an easy head start. By the time the first shouts came up behind him, he'd already covered a good hundred yards or more.

But that lead couldn't last forever. Even on a good day, he'd never outpace a group of Nukula through the woods. If there were such a thing as a home-field advantage, they definitely had it.

Maybe he'd be caught. A million punishments might be coming his way. But none of that mattered more than getting to Jane, Vanessa, and Buzz. He kept his chin down, his eyes on the ground, and his feet moving.

Finally, when his lungs felt ready to burst, Carter stopped and took a knee in the tall grass. His own heart pounded in his ears, but he could still hear the drums from the east, too. That was good.

And then another sound emerged. Rushing water. Even better.

His paper-dry throat clenched. He hadn't noticed how desperate he was for a drink until now. The sound of the river, if that's what it was, came from just ahead and to the left. If anything was worth making a run for, this was it.

He stood up and took off again, heading toward the sound. Before long, the forest thinned enough to show him the rolling white breakers of a riverbed. The water was flowing east, but it looked dangerous, like a highway of rapids and boulders as far as Carter could see.

Still, this was a way out. Maybe he couldn't outrun the others, but he could ride the river as fast as anyone. If he was lucky, he'd be washed straight downstream.

If he was unlucky, he'd get smashed against one of those rocks.

Or even worse, he'd wind up held under by a recirculating current. It was called the washing machine effect. He'd heard about it when the family went rafting on the Wolf River in Wisconsin. That was the last thing you wanted if you fell into rapids. Once that happened, drowning was the easy part.

Before there was time to think anymore, a shout came up from the woods. Someone was coming.

Another shout, even closer, was all the push Carter needed. With a deep breath, he waded in, picked up his feet, and let the river take him.

The current pulled him along even faster than he'd expected. For several seconds, he was underwater, rising and falling with the river's swells. As soon as he left one stretch of white water behind, he was into the next.

It was all a blur until a fallen tree caught him up short. Branches scratched at his arms and legs, and across his face, until he managed to land a hand on one of the sturdier limbs.

His fingers closed around the moss-slick bark. There was no getting a firm grip, but it slowed him down. He slid several more feet, until his hand lodged into the crook between two branches. His body jerked to a stop, and a sharp pain ran up his arm.

Still, the water was rushing over his head. He needed air—now. Carter reached around blindly for something else to hold on to, anything he could grab to get himself above the surface. He found a second branch, which snapped off, but then another that held. It was enough to let him shift his weight and free his stuck hand. Then he pulled himself up and out for a quick gulp of air.

He could see the bank now. And there, clear enough, were three of the runners he'd left behind at the mouth of the gorge. They hadn't seen him. Not yet. They were scanning the river and the woods on the far side.

Carter kept as low as he could. The rise and fall of the water hid him from view, but he couldn't stay here much longer. His grip wasn't going to last, and the river seemed to want nothing more than to suck him farther downstream.

Carter squeezed his eyes shut. He focused every thought on his hands.

Hold on. Don't let go. Hold on. . . .

He just had to keep this position for a few more seconds. Just until the others turned away. Why were they taking so long to move on? His hand cramped. He could feel it giving way.

One of the runners on the bank pointed into the woods. The others looked in that direction, and they all turned to run farther upstream.

Half a second later, Carter's fingers slipped free. He was moving again, tossing through swells and dips like a piece of driftwood as he scraped past one unseen rock after another. The river was carrying him east, anyway. But that didn't mean he was safe.

It didn't even mean he was going to survive this.

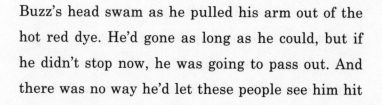

Buzz's head swam as he pulled his arm out of the hot red dye. He'd gone as long as he could, but if he didn't stop now, he was going to pass out. And there was no way he'd let these people see him hit the dirt. Everyone else had stayed on their feet including Vanessa, who had finished first. If they could get through it, Buzz thought, so would he.

"You did well," Ani said. With three flicks of his stone knife, he cut the cords around Buzz's screen and let it drop to the floor.

His whole arm tingled. He stared at the pattern left behind on his skin—red diamond shapes, bigger around his shoulder and smaller toward the wrist. It was like the full-sleeve tattoos he'd seen on lots of people back home. But never on kids. And definitely never on someone like him, an eleven-year-old gamer who didn't exactly have a reputation for being tough. Not before all this, anyway.

Jane eased her arm out next. Her face was wet with sweat, but not tears. At nine years old, she was the youngest one out here, but nobody complained less than Jane.

That left only Mima. All of the others had finished. She stayed steadfast, up to her armpit in the hot liquid. Her eyes were like glass. Her mouth was set in a line that showed no emotion, no pain. Buzz had never known anyone so unafraid of anything as her.

For years, Mima had lived as an outcast among the Nukula, ever since her parents had committed the unpardonable crime of trying to leave the tribe. They'd paid with their lives in the island's killer tides and left behind a daughter whose only chance for redemption was *Raku Nau* itself.

Now, with a *seccu* around her neck, Mima had a chance to claim her place as an adult in the tribe. Even Laki watched with approving eyes while Mima gutted it out longer than anyone.

Up to now, the marking ceremony had taken place in silence. All Buzz heard was the hiss and spitting of the fire. But a sudden commotion from overhead seemed to fill the room with noise. Several people were moving through the jungle nearby. And then a voice came down through the foliage-covered bamboo ceiling. Whoever it was sounded urgent, but the only word Buzz understood was "Chizo."

Before the messenger had even finished, Laki was on the move. He headed up the tunnel toward the canoes and *Trehila*. Ani whispered to Mima, who slowly pulled her arm out of the dye, as all of the others began to follow the chief out of the arena.

"Chizo has arrived on the eastern shore," Ani told them. "He will be sent straight to the top of *Trehila*, while the tribe witnesses his exile."

"How long does he have to stay up there?" Vanessa asked.

"Perhaps for a season or more. Perhaps a year," Ani said.

"A *year*?" Jane asked.

"I never thought I could feel sorry for him," Vanessa said, "But—"

"Don't even," Buzz interrupted her.

Buzz had been the one taken captive by Chizo, in the midst of *Raku Nau*. He was the one who'd been tied up and attacked by an army of fire ants while Chizo watched, and even laughed. Sympathy was the last thing on Buzz's mind right now.

"Come on," he said, and moved toward the tunnel behind all the others. "I don't want to miss this."

Everyone had gathered at the base of *Trehila* by the time Vanessa, Buzz, Jane, Mima, and Ani got there. The giant screen still stood in the closed position, but Chizo was there now, along with the two guards Laki had sent to retrieve him.

Vanessa had never noticed how much Chizo and Laki looked alike. Chizo seemed to be pleading with his father, from the way his voice went up and the way he kept trying to catch Laki's eye.

Laki stood with his hands behind his back, staring at the ocean as though Chizo wasn't even there. A few murmured to Laki from the side, but he ignored them, too.

Finally, Chizo stopped trying. He turned away from Laki and stepped onto the first rung of the vine ladder that ran to the top of *Trehila*. As he did, Laki broke his own silence with a single word.

"Shesto!" he said.

Chizo slowly turned back to look at Laki again, and Laki held out a hand. His palm was flat, as though he was expecting something.

"Ma betta e tikko fotza, Chizo!" Laki said.

Several in the crowd gasped, but not Chizo. Without a word, he slipped a small ring off his left pinkie and dropped it into his father's hand. The ring was wood, or maybe bone. Vanessa couldn't tell from where she stood. As soon as Chizo had given it up, he turned once more and started his climb without looking back.

"That was the blood ring," Ani said quietly. "It marked Chizo as Laki's son."

"And now . . . he's not?" Jane asked.

Ani shook his head. "This has never happened before" was all he said.

While everyone watched, Chizo moved quickly up the side of the huge palm. Soon, he was above the jungle canopy, lit by the westward sunlight that streamed over the other treetops. It was scary to watch him go so high. There were no jacklines, no safety nets, and nothing but the vine ladder to hold on to as he followed the curve of the tree, all the way out over the water.

When he reached the tiny guard hut built into *Trehila*'s crown, he maneuvered onto the platform and disappeared. Almost right away, another boy appeared and started his own climb down.

It was a strange turn of events, Vanessa thought. Just as Mima was finding a place in the tribe, Chizo was losing his, exiled by his own father. The Nukula had their own customs, that was for sure. But if the faces of the other tribe members were any clue, not everyone here seemed to approve of this choice.

And already, something else was happening. The climbing boy had barely started down when Chizo's voice rang out from the top of the tree. The climber stopped and looked, then pointed toward the beach with one hand.

Vanessa peered out through the gaps in the big screen. A swimmer had just arrived on the shore. It was the female elder who had followed them through *Raku Nau*. Now she was running toward them and yelling some sort of announcement to the tribe.

Or maybe it was a warning. When Vanessa looked to Ani, even he seemed concerned. Laki motioned the woman over while everyone else began to buzz and chatter.

"What is it?" Jane asked. "What's going on?"

"It is your brother," Ani said.

Vanessa's breath caught in her throat. "Carter?" she said. "Is he okay?" All kinds of possibilities ran through her mind before Ani could even answer.

"He has run off," Ani said, just as Laki boomed out a single word to the assembled tribe.

"Ohzooka!" he shouted.

And everything changed again.

CHAPTER 6

"Ani, what's happening?" Buzz said. "What's *oh-zoo*—"

"*Ohzooka*," Ani said. "It is a hunt. The last time it was declared was the day you came to the island."

Jane shuddered just thinking about it. The pit Vanessa had fallen into when they landed on Shadow Island had seemed like the end of the road. Then Jane and Carter had been taken as well. It was part of the young Nukulas' training, to capture them, but there was no knowing that at the time.

Everything was happening so fast. All of the tribe's new leaders—those Nukula who had earned the *seccu* that day—gathered around Laki. He held the blood ring over his head and continued to address the group.

Mima looked back once, but Ani waved her on to join the others. Then he spoke to Jane, Vanessa, and Buzz in a fast burst of instructions.

"Listen to me," Ani said. "Nothing about today has gone as expected. Laki is offering the blood ring to anyone who will bring Carter here to the eastern shore. This is an opportunity, and you must seize it."

"An opportunity for . . . what, exactly?" Buzz asked. "To get that ring? To lead the tribe? That's crazy!"

Ani's mouth shut tight. But for Jane, even his silence had something to say, and it wasn't about winning the blood ring.

"This is our chance to find Carter and get away!" she said. Now Ani looked at her approvingly, and she kept going. "We can escape! If we can find him first—"

"How are we going to do that?" Buzz asked, nervously eyeing the thirteen other runners.

"I don't know," Jane said. "But we have to. This is our chance."

Ani spoke up again. "If your brother is trying to reach you—"

"He is," Jane said. There was no doubt in her mind.

"—then he will travel in this direction," Ani said. He pointed across to Cloud Ridge but pivoted to the right, indicating the curve of land around the bay. "It is the narrowest part of the island. The ground is not easy to navigate there. In places, it is impossible. That is why the tribe travels here by water."

"But Carter doesn't know any of that," Vanessa said. "He's just running blind, straight toward it."

"Yes," Ani said simply. The Nukula always seemed to take obstacles as facts, not problems.

So maybe it was time to start thinking like a Nukula, Jane thought.

"What happens if someone else finds him?" she asked.

"I suspect Laki will leave him here when we depart for the village tomorrow," Ani said.

"We can't be separated!" Vanessa said. "Not again. I won't let it happen."

"Then do not fail," Ani said.

He wasn't going to tell them to disobey Laki, Jane realized. Not exactly. But if they could get to Carter first, and get him back here to the eastern shore without anyone seeing, at least they'd have a chance for escape. One *last* chance.

Now Ani looked upstream, along the channel to where the boats were tethered. "My canoe has a small store of coconuts and water on board," he told them.

"But . . . we can't take your canoe," Jane said. "It's yours."

"It is mine to give," Ani answered.

Even now, he hadn't told them what to do. He was only stating facts. This was an opportunity. His canoe held some supplies. It was his boat to give.

What they did with those facts was up to them. And even then, it was a terrible risk Ani was taking. His own place in the tribe could be threatened if they betrayed his trust in any way.

"Whatever happens, it will be decided by sunrise," Ani added. "That is how much time you have."

Jane looked up. Already, the light was turning gold

and orange with the end of the day. Before long, night would set in.

"How are we going to do this?" Buzz asked. "We can't compete against these guys. They're going to leave us in the dust."

"We got this far, didn't we?" Jane asked.

"Yeah. With Mima's help," Buzz said.

"What's Mima doing?" Vanessa asked.

Mima was still with the other group of *seccu* winners, waiting for the start of *Ohzooka*. She knelt on the ground, sharpening a smaller rock against a boulder for a makeshift blade. Already, she'd broken off a crude handle from a piece of bamboo. Everyone was working fast to get ready—cutting and coiling vines, gauging the landscape, and speaking low with their family members.

For all of them, it was about more than just a hunt now. It was about earning the blood ring, and securing a place of leadership in the tribe.

"Mima will run her own *Ohzooka*," Ani said. "You must allow her that."

"But we need her," Buzz said. "We're a team. She

wouldn't have even gotten to the end if it wasn't for Carter! She owes us!"

"If it wasn't for Mima, we never would have made it that far to begin with," Jane said. It made sense, at least to her. This was a chance for Mima to turn her life around beyond anything she'd probably imagined. And who was to say Mima's life was any less important than their lives?

There was nothing more to do about it, anyway. Mima was as stubborn as Carter. If she'd decided to run this alone, then that was that.

"When does it start?" Vanessa asked.

"Immediately," Ani said, raising his chin in Laki's direction.

Laki stood in the middle of the group, his hand raised high over his head, with the small blood ring grasped in his fingers. He called out then, in a long, sustained note. As he did, everyone stopped what they were doing and turned to face west.

With no more warning than that, Laki's call ended, his hand came down to his side, and the group of runners sprang into motion.

This was it—the beginning of *Ohzooka*.

The hunt for Carter was on.

It was amazing, the way the Nukula runners took to the trees. Within seconds, the canopy was full of people moving from branch to limb, to the ground, and back up into the next tree again—all heading west.

"What do we do now?" Jane asked.

"Mima!" Vanessa shouted, but Mima was already gone.

Maybe it was even for the best, Buzz thought. She could travel faster without them. At least that meant they had an ally at the front of the pack. And none of them—Buzz, Jane, Vanessa, or even Carter, who was the strongest—had come anywhere near mastering the *parkour*-like moves of the Nukula.

"We're losing them already!" Jane said as they pushed into the forest. "Come on! We have to try!"

"Hang on a second!" Vanessa said.

Buzz turned to look. Vanessa's gaze pivoted inland. Her eyebrows knit together.

"What is it?" Buzz asked.

"This way!" she said, and crashed through the brush ahead of them.

"Vanessa? Where are you going?" Jane asked.

Vanessa looked around before she answered. None of the other runners spoke English, but still, she only mouthed the words.

To the tunnels, she said.

The one advantage of being behind the pack was that nobody noticed as they veered to an alternate route. Vanessa led the way, pushing a rough path through the tall brush that Buzz and Jane could follow. It wasn't easy going, but she seemed to be onto something. And right now, a fast, risky decision was better than no decision at all. If one of those tunnels headed in the right direction, at least they'd have some chance of catching up to the others.

"Vanessa!" Jane said before they'd gone too far. "What about the guards?"

Vanessa stopped short, breathing hard as she turned. "You're right," she said. "We don't know if they'll stop us or not."

"But that guard hut isn't the only way in," Buzz said.

"Do you mean the other tunnels?" Jane asked. "We don't have time to get all the way over—"

"No," Buzz said. "Not the other tunnels. There's something else we can try."

He brushed past his sisters and moved into the lead, taking them in a slightly new direction. The scratch of the brambles and undergrowth on his legs was nothing new. Buzz ignored it as he pushed farther into the woods.

Before long, the domed bamboo ceiling that covered the underground chamber came into sight. They looked at one another in the silence as they approached it. Maybe there were guards at the hut nearby, and maybe there weren't. But the safest bet right now was to move as quietly as possible.

Buzz parted some of the brush that grew over the bamboo to look down inside. The place was empty. He scanned the arena, looking for a vine that grew all the way to the dirt floor inside.

That's the way in, he mouthed to his sisters.

Vanessa and Jane both nodded back. They understood.

Buzz pointed to himself and then down in again. *I'll go first,* he told them.

The ceiling's bamboo crosspieces were laid close together. Even the widest gaps looked small for squeezing through. And he was the heaviest of them all. If he couldn't fit, he'd have to send the girls on without him.

You'll fit, Jane mouthed, as if reading his thoughts, or at least his expression.

Buzz wasn't so sure, but worrying was just one more way to waste time. He could hear the other runners crashing through the forest and heading farther west by the minute.

He sat himself on the first crossbar of bamboo and swung his legs over to dangle his feet inside. The ground was more than a story below, maybe even two stories. Falling could mean a broken leg, or worse. And there was no knowing if these vines would hold his weight, even if he did squeeze through.

With another deep breath, he leaned in and gripped

the longest vine he could spot. There was no turning back now.

Sliding forward, he was surprised to feel his belly slip right through the gap. In fact, there wasn't much belly left. Not after eating so little for so many days. The painful scrape of his ribs against the bamboo told him so.

For a fraction of a second, he dropped. Then the vine snapped taut in his hands and he swung crazily back and forth. As he did, he lowered himself toward the ground, hand over hand with all the strength he could muster.

It didn't last. He was halfway down when his grip gave out. The woody vine tore into his palms like a million splinters before he dropped the last several feet to the dirt below. It wasn't pretty, but he was in. He rubbed his palms to put out the fiery feeling, and motioned to the girls to go for it.

Jane was the monkey of the group. She managed to lower herself all the way without any trouble. Vanessa climbed and then slid, like Buzz had done.

That way? Vanessa mouthed. She pointed down

the tunnel that led directly under the guard hut.

Jane and Buzz nodded. The tunnel definitely set out to the west, but it was impossible to say how far it went, or what kind of turns it might take. From where they stood, it was just a black hole.

The only thing to compare it to was the tunnel leading in the opposite direction, toward *Trehila* and the canoes. That one had been a straight shot, and not very long. But it didn't mean this one would be the same way. Which was the whole point. They had no idea.

Here! Jane indicated, and bent down to pick up an abandoned torch from the marking ceremony. She used it to stir the ashes in the fire pit and quickly turned up a few orange embers. Soon after that, they had a small flame to carry with them.

Jane went first, with Buzz and Vanessa close behind. They moved cautiously past the ladder that led up to the guard hut, and then picked up their pace over the uneven tunnel floor, continuing west.

Hopefully, toward Carter.

CHAPTER 7

The light was dimming fast when Carter stumbled onto the mud bank of the river. He'd ridden the current as far as he could. Now, the water had slowed to a near standstill, and gone shallow.

There was no knowing how far he'd come. It was all a blur of white water, rock, and mud. Both his knees were bloody, and he'd have some new bruises for sure, but at least nothing was broken.

He stood on the bank and listened. The jungle gave back its usual insect buzz and hum, and he could hear the soft sound of ocean waves somewhere. The drumming from the eastern shore had stopped.

He was completely turned around now, with no real sense of direction.

Carter turned and looked for the sun. It was too late in the day for that, but through the trees behind him, he could make out the red-orange glow of a sunset. That meant west, didn't it? His mind felt thick and slow. He needed food. Fresh water. Rest. But he couldn't have any of those things.

It was tempting to drop right there in the mud and close his eyes. Falling asleep would have been beyond easy. But the darkening sky was like a ticking clock he couldn't afford to ignore. So he put the sunset at his back and pushed on, one step at a time.

His path took him over a small rise through the forest and back down again, into a patch of wetter and muddier ground. The river hadn't dried up so much as fed into a swamp of some kind.

The island around him had narrowed, too. He could see the ocean, first on his left and soon after on his right. But his pace was miserable. The ground was just a murky slime under his tattered sneakers. It felt like walking through wet cement.

With the next step, he was up to his calf in scum-covered water. He stumbled, caught himself on the trunk of a dead tree, and kept moving.

Jane . . .

Buzz . . .

Vanessa . . .

Mima . . .

Their names passed through his mind, over and over. Each name was a step. It was all he had to keep him moving as the darkness deepened around him. And for now, that would have to be enough.

Vanessa peered into the tunnel ahead. It felt as though they were still heading west, but it was hard to say. At least there were no choices to make, no forks or turns to choose from. The passage cut a single straight path, wherever it was taking them.

"Carter wouldn't head back for the village, would he?" Buzz asked.

"Not if he's thinking straight," Vanessa said. But that was no guarantee with Carter. He usually made decisions first and thought second, if at all. "We don't know anything for sure," she added.

"I do," Jane said. "He's coming for us."

Jane had known Carter all her life, the same way Buzz and Vanessa had known each other all of their lives. It was only a few months ago that they'd all become brothers and sisters. And Jane sounded as sure of herself now as she'd ever been.

Soon, the soft thudding of their footsteps turned into a wet slapping sound. The ground was becoming muddier as they traveled west. The idea of rats and other animals scratched at Vanessa's mind, too. But there was nothing they could do about that. Hopefully, they were alone down here.

"Where is this *going*?" Buzz asked, the frustration heavy in his voice. Nobody answered. All they could do now was stick with the gamble they'd made.

After several more minutes, something showed in the dark up ahead. It was just a ragged crack of light, but Vanessa nearly cried when she saw it.

"Do you see that?" she asked, and they all hurried toward it.

They seemed to be traveling uphill. By the time they came to the tunnel's dead end, Vanessa could touch the dripping, rocky ceiling. And there, just above their heads, was the crevice of light they'd been moving toward. She pressed her fingers into it and felt around.

"There's a rock here," she said. "A big one. Give me a hand."

Jane stepped back to let Buzz through and held the torch up to shed some light. The flame was tiny by now. It wouldn't last much longer.

Vanessa held her breath while she and Buzz pressed their hands flat against the small boulder and pushed. It rocked away from them once, then thudded back into place.

"Again!" Buzz said. "Jane, help!"

The torch was down to a tiny match light by now, and it went out completely when Jane set it down. Vanessa's adrenaline surged in the dark. With the next push, the rock rolled away from her hands, leaving behind a hole just big enough to climb through.

"I'll go," she said, and scurried out.

She came into a small alcove of some kind, with curved woody walls on either side. They were close enough that she had to wriggle forward just to get free of the small space.

And in fact, they weren't walls, she realized. They were the tall roots of a tree, like the banyans back in the Nukula village. The rock they'd moved had clearly been wedged in there to block the tunnel's entrance. Or maybe to hide it.

Buzz came right behind. He turned around then and lay flat on his stomach to help pull Jane out while Vanessa scanned their new surroundings.

They'd arrived in a marshland. The ground where they stood was one big mud puddle. Straight ahead was a large pool, mostly covered in green scum and ringed with more of the same odd trees. Their lower branches were heavy with thick moss that hung like old tattered sheets out to dry.

It would be getting dark soon, Vanessa realized. In fact, the days were getting just a bit shorter. It was hard to believe they'd been in the South Pacific for over three weeks—long enough for something like that to change. But they had. She tried to remember the last time she'd even looked at a clock.

The outside world was slipping away, bit by bit. And from the look of the dead, empty landscape around them, so were their chances of ever getting out of here.

"This is exactly what Ani told us about," Jane said. "He told us we'd be crossing the island's narrowest point. That has to be here, don't you think?"

The land had thinned to no more than a few hundred yards across. She could see the ocean in both directions. It seemed as though the Nukula had dug the westward tunnel as far as they could. Any farther and it would be underwater.

"Do you think Carter could have gotten this far already?" Vanessa asked.

"I doubt it," Buzz said. "He's got to still be coming this way, right?"

"Right," Jane said. But it was nothing more than a guess. That was all they had.

Continuing west through the swamp was going to

be exhausting. That much was clear. Still, however tired and hungry Jane felt, she knew Carter had to feel worse. At least she, Vanessa, and Buzz had been given some water and a tiny bit of rest. Their brother didn't have that advantage.

Suddenly, Vanessa clutched Jane's shoulder.

"Someone's over there!" she said.

"Who?" Jane said, looking around. "Where?"

"I see her," Buzz said, and pointed straight into the marsh. "Up there."

And then Jane saw her, too. The girl was sitting on the lowermost branch of a dead tree in the middle of the swamp. The vine she'd brought was coiled over her shoulder, and she seemed to be tying one end of it into a loop.

She was setting a trap, Jane realized. For Carter.

"And there!" Buzz whispered, pointing off to the right this time.

"And there, too! Behind us!" Vanessa said.

The more Jane peered around the marsh, the more of them she saw. It was like a seek-and-find puzzle, one shadow after another emerging from the gloom.

In the twilight, it was hard to tell the boys from the girls, or if Mima was among them.

Everyone seemed to be betting on the same thing. If Carter was heading east, he'd have to cross this narrow land bridge. And that's where *someone* was going to capture him.

Jane's heart sank. They'd made up some ground, but it almost didn't matter. How were they supposed to find Carter first, much less get him back to the eastern shore in secret?

Unless. . . .

"What now?" Vanessa asked. "Any ideas?"

"Even if we can find him, everyone's going to know about it," Buzz said.

"That's true," Jane said. "I was thinking the same thing, but . . ." An idea was flickering to life in her mind.

"What is it?" Vanessa asked.

"Well . . ." she said. She squeezed her eyes shut, thinking it through. "We have to figure out something we can do that they can't. Or something we have that they don't."

"Okay?" Buzz said. "Keep going."

"They're all hiding and staying as quiet as possible, right?" Jane said. "What if we do the opposite?"

"What does that even mean?" Vanessa asked.

"This," Jane said. Then she took a deep breath and screamed their brother's name as loud as she possibly could.

CHAPTER 8

Buzz froze. He couldn't believe what he was hearing from Jane.

"CARTER!" she screamed. "IF YOU CAN HEAR ME, DON'T SAY ANYTHING! *DO NOT SAY ANYTHING!* JUST LISTEN!"

The swamp seemed to echo with her voice. Everything else was still.

"Are you crazy?" Vanessa yelled. She grabbed Jane by both arms. "What are you doing?"

"The only thing we can!" Jane said, not even trying to quiet down. "CARTER, IF YOU CAN HEAR ME, THERE ARE PEOPLE HERE TRYING TO CATCH

YOU. STAY OUT OF SIGHT, AND LISTEN TO MY VOICE!"

Buzz stared at her hard. He trusted Jane, but he didn't understand.

"Jane?" he said.

"If Carter's coming through here, there's literally no way for us to get to him without people noticing," she explained. "So maybe he can get to us."

"What good does that do?" Vanessa asked. "Everyone knows we're here."

"That's the point," Jane said. "First, we create as much of a distraction as we can. And then we get Carter into that tunnel. It seems like we're the only ones out here right now who know about it. That's worth a lot."

"Yeah, but the tunnel's pitch-black," Buzz said. "Without any fire, what good does it do us now?"

"It would be hard to get back that way, but not impossible," Jane said. "Remember the caves on Nowhere Island?"

They'd all had to feel their way through the pitch-black before. It had been one of the hardest things they'd done, but they'd made it through.

"Carter can do this," Jane added. "I know he can."

"Hang on," Buzz said. "Why just Carter?"

Jane put a hand over her eyes. She seemed to be making up parts of the plan with every new second.

"We'll . . . tell him where the tunnel is," she said. "If Carter can get back and stay out of sight underground until we find him, then we can try to sneak him over to Ani's canoe. Everyone else is going to have to go back by land at some point, and we'll follow them that way. Or we'll find our own way—"

"Hang on," Vanessa said. "Do you know how many things you just named that could go wrong?"

"What if Carter isn't anywhere near here?" Buzz said. "We don't even know if he can hear us."

"We'll keep yelling for him, over and over," Jane said. "All night, if we have to. Ani's the only other one on this island who speaks English."

"What if one of the guards finds him at the other end?" Vanessa said. "Or one of the elders?"

Jane took an impatient breath. "And what if someone here finds him first?" she said. "And what if the tide rises and fills the tunnel with water? And what if *anything,* you guys! Do either of you have a better idea? Because I sure would like to hear it!"

Buzz swallowed hard. He felt stunned, the same way Jane looked. She'd never taken charge like this, or even spoken to them so forcefully.

"One more thing," she said. "We should spread out. Buzz and I can keep going into the swamp near the others. Vanessa, see if you can roll that rock back to hide the tunnel after we're gone. We'll try to distract everyone so they don't see you doing it. Then you should move away from it, too. We don't want to be anywhere near it if Carter . . . well, hopefully *when* Carter gets this far."

"Got it," Buzz said.

Maybe Jane's idea was crazy, or maybe it was brilliant, but they had to go with it. This was about what they could do *right now,* because there wasn't anything else.

Without another word, they moved out. Jane went left. Buzz went right. Vanessa hung back. And then Jane started up, yelling all over again.

"CARTER! IF YOU CAN HEAR MY VOICE . . ."

". . . DON'T SAY ANYTHING! JUST LISTEN! THERE ARE PEOPLE HERE LOOKING FOR YOU . . ."

Carter couldn't believe his ears. It was Jane, coming from somewhere ahead. Somewhere not that far off. How was this even happening?

"STAY OUT OF SIGHT, AND IF YOU CAN COME THIS WAY, DO IT. THERE'S A TUNNEL YOU HAVE TO FIND, NEAR VANESSA."

And then Vanessa's voice was there.

"CARTER, THIS WAY!" she shouted from a different place. "IF YOU CAN HEAR ME, LOOK FOR THE BIG TREE ON THE EDGE OF THE SWAMP. THE TUNNEL ENTRANCE IS RIGHT THERE, UNDER A BIG ROCK. THAT'S WHERE YOU NEED TO GO!"

"JUST KEEP LISTENING!" Buzz shouted from another direction. "AND KEEP TRYING TO MOVE TOWARD VANESSA. JANE AND I ARE GOING TO MAKE AS MUCH OF A DIVERSION AS WE CAN!"

Of course, Carter thought. He was the only one who could understand them. Mima knew a few English words, but Mima wasn't their problem right now. Everyone else was.

It was starting to make sense, and it was incredibly smart. This was probably Jane's idea. Just the sound of their voices flooded him with relief and gave him a surge of energy, too.

And then they started over, with all of the same instructions.

"CARTER! IF YOU CAN HEAR MY VOICE, DON'T SAY ANYTHING!" Jane screamed. "JUST LISTEN . . ."

Jane and Buzz were on the move, from the sound of it. And Carter needed to be, too. But carefully.

He took a deep breath. Going slow wasn't his strong suit. Still, he crouched down and tried to get a read on the landscape before he did anything else.

Through the swamp, maybe fifty yards ahead, he spotted two runners. One was stringing vines between two trees. The other was pushing through the bog, up to his chest in the scummy water. He spoke to a third

Nukula as he passed, someone Carter hadn't even noticed until that moment.

The Nukula were masters of camouflage and not being seen. That much Carter knew. And maybe he could take a page from their playbook.

He crept backward and took a position behind one of the half-dead trees that grew all around. There was no shortage of mud here, and he scooped up two big handfuls. It went onto his arms, his legs, his face— even his clothes and hair—like a paste.

The whole time, Vanessa, Jane, and Buzz were shouting themselves hoarse, repeating the same ideas over and over.

"CARTER, IF YOU CAN HEAR ME . . ."

"FOLLOW MY VOICE . . ."

"THERE'S A TUNNEL . . ."

I hear you, I hear you! He wanted to yell it out more than anything. Instead, he stayed out of sight behind the tree and stood up slowly. Reaching a little higher, he pulled down a thick sheet of the gray moss that grew over the tree's branches. Most of it crumbled away in his hands, but it left enough to do one arm.

And there was plenty more where that came from.

Working as quickly as he could, he plastered himself in a rough coat of the moss. Hopefully, between that and the oncoming darkness, he'd have the cover he needed to get across the bog. A lot of the moss would wash away in the water, but there was nothing he could do about that. All he could really do was stay low, move carefully, and keep his eyes open.

Carter scanned a full 360 one more time. The nearest runner he could spot was still a good distance off. This was his chance to get going.

He lowered himself all the way to the ground. He took a breath for focus. And then he started a silent, methodical crawl toward the sound of his sister's voice.

Jane moved deeper into the swamp, pulling her feet through the thick, muddy bottom. The water was up to her chest now. She couldn't see Buzz anymore, either, but she could hear him. Both of them kept calling out, giving Carter instructions and creating as much distraction for the other runners as they could.

"THERE'S ONE IN A TREE RIGHT ABOVE ME!" she shouted.

"TWO MORE OVER HERE!" Buzz answered back. "ONE OF THEM'S STILL HEADING WEST."

"I THINK IT'S ALL CLEAR HERE!" Vanessa shouted. "BUT CARTER, IF YOU CAN HEAR US, PLEASE BE CAREFUL! THEY COULD BE ANYWHERE!"

It felt good to scream, just to let off some of the nervous energy inside. Meanwhile, Jane forced herself *not* to look back in Vanessa's direction. If Carter was moving that way, they needed to keep everyone else's focus away from the tunnel.

They'd definitely gotten some attention. Above her, a Nukula boy sat on a branch, looking down as she passed. He said something to her that sounded angry, but she ignored him and kept moving as though she knew exactly where she was going. Two others had begun to follow her, too, not even trying to hide anymore.

"ANY OF YOU GUYS SEE MIMA ANYWHERE?" Vanessa called over.

"NOT YET!" Buzz called back.

"ME, NEITHER!" Jane answered. It would have been completely like Mima to continue west and separate herself from the larger group. But it was impossible to know where she was.

I hope you're out there somewhere, Mima. Please, help us if you can.

The longer it all went on, the more Nukula voices started cropping up around the swamp. They all seemed confused now, which was good news. It was no guarantee, but it gave Jane, Buzz, and Vanessa more to work with than they'd had a few minutes earlier.

And right now, they needed any advantage they could get.

CHAPTER 9

Carter slid through the swamp one step at a time, keeping low in the water. His head was still covered with a makeshift hood of the moss, and he probably looked like something out of a scary movie, he thought. Or better yet, he'd look like nothing at all and blend right into the bog around him.

The whole idea was to stay as far from any of the Nukula as he could manage. It reminded him of something Dad had said before, about getting downfield in a game. *Go where the other guys aren't.* It was so simple, but so true.

Of course, it was a whole lot easier when the other

team wasn't practically invisible in the dark. But it was something to think about, anyway.

"CARTER, IF YOU CAN HEAR ME . . ." Jane started up again. This time, she was off to his left.

"CARTER!" Buzz yelled from farther off. "HEAD TOWARD VANESSA!"

"OVER HERE! CARTER!" Vanessa's voice followed theirs. "THE ENTRANCE TO THE TUNNEL IS BETWEEN THE ROOTS OF A BIG TREE."

He could hear them talking to each other, too.

"How long should we do this?" Buzz asked from wherever he was.

"I don't know," Jane called back. "As long as we can. Carter wouldn't give up on us, and we can't give up on him."

It was a bizarre feeling to know they were right there, yet to stay perfectly still. Everything in him wanted to jump up and race over to Jane.

Instead, he waited like a statue for several minutes until the one Nukula boy he could spot had moved on. Then Carter pointed himself east again and continued toward the far side of the deep pool.

Finally, straight ahead, he saw it. The water gave way to a muddy shore, and beyond that, a tree sat with a large rock wedged between its roots. That had to be it.

As he moved into the shallower water, he sank down even more, bending his knees at first, then lying flat when he had to. He pulled himself along by his hands now, with only his eyes and the top of his head breaking the surface.

When he couldn't go any farther without standing up, he stopped again. There was just a short patch of open ground between him and the tree he was trying to reach. That meant one more big move, if he could manage to make it without being seen.

But that was a big *if*.

Vanessa's skin prickled when she saw Carter at the water's edge. He was maybe fifty feet off to her left, and less than half that distance from the tunnel entrance.

It was amazing. Jane's plan was actually working!

She turned to face west again, her heart racing. It was too risky to look Carter's way for very long. There was no knowing who was watching who out here.

"Jane? Buzz?" she called out. "I think he's here. I don't want to say too much, but Carter, I can see you. Don't look around. Just keep going. As far as I can tell, you're clear to go. The tree's straight ahead. It's the one with the rock between the roots."

She cut her eyes over one more time. It was hard to tell in the dim light, but it looked as though Carter was nodding.

"Jane?" she called again. "Buzz? Don't do anything. Just wait."

"Got it!" Buzz yelled.

"You can do it, Carter!" Jane called back.

But then Vanessa heard a Nukula voice, too. It came out of the dark, closer in than Jane or Buzz. *"Runaka, okolo!"* the boy said.

Then another. *"Betta eh fatzo, tikka-ko, tikka!"*

That was followed quickly by splashing and footsteps, all of it coming closer.

"They may have spotted him!" Vanessa reported.

"Carter. Just go! I can't see them, but hurry if you can!"

"HEY! HEY! HEY!" Jane yelled from her place in the bog. "OVER HERE, EVERYONE! OVER HERE!"

"OVER HERE!" Buzz yelled, picking up Jane's cue. It was more important than ever to keep everyone else distracted.

Vanessa held her breath. She watched as Carter came onto his feet and made a low run toward the tunnel entrance. It was too dark to see much, but the others were definitely moving in, and fast.

This was going to be close.

CHAPTER 10

Carter's feet slipped over the mud as he tried to get some traction. He stumbled, went down, scrambled back up, and kept moving.

This was it. He'd either make it to the tunnel or he wouldn't.

In a second he'd reached the big rock between the roots of the tree. He threw his arms over the top of it and heaved. The rock pulled away in one fast motion. His exhaustion was nothing. Right now, adrenaline was everything.

Before he could make his next move, another yell came from much closer, this time in Nukula.

"Runaka! Betzo aztet! Runaka looko!"

"CARTER, WATCH OUT!" Vanessa shouted.

He froze. Should he keep going? Try to disappear into the tunnel? Run back to the swamp?

"OVER HERE!" Buzz yelled. "OVER HERE!" He was trying to keep up the diversion, but it was too late.

Carter turned to see several shadows closing in. He bent his knees and put his hands up, ready to tackle his way out of this if he had to. But before any of the others could get there, a vine loop dropped into his field of vision. He noticed it at the same moment it slipped around his head.

Carter reached up to snatch the vine off, too late. It already had him, and pulled up tight under his chin.

Someone dropped from a branch overhead. The slack in the vine went even tighter, and nearly yanked Carter off his feet. Whoever it was hit the ground behind him and snaked both arms around his shoulders. The loop tightened again, cutting into his windpipe.

Carter's first thought was *Chizo*. But it couldn't be. Or could it?

He twisted around trying to see just as his attacker threw him to the ground—but not before he got a glimpse of her face.

It was Mima.

Jane was rushing back toward the shallow water when she saw it happen. Mima dropped from the tree, holding one end of a vine. The other end looped over the limb she'd left behind and back down to where it had Carter by the neck.

Mima landed on him and brought him up with both hands around his shoulders. There was a fast tussle, even as all of the others closed in from several directions.

"CARTER!" Jane screamed. She didn't stop as she ran out of the water and right to him, squeezing through the group to get to her brother.

"FAH!" Mima reached out with one hand and knocked Jane straight back.

Jane stumbled and fell hard in the mud. The shock of the hit was as strong as anything she'd felt since coming to this place. Her mind reeled, trying to make sense of what was happening. Did Mima think she was someone else?

Buzz and Vanessa were there now, too. Several Nukula were trying to take Carter for themselves, but Mima was having none of it. She screeched at them all, and slashed at the air with her stone knife in a warning. It brought the chaos to a fast standstill, and everyone backed up.

"Carter!" Jane tried again from where she stood.

Carter didn't move. He couldn't. When he tried to turn toward Jane, he coughed and gagged. Mima had drawn up the slack in the vine, keeping herself between him and everyone else. Now she turned and cut the vine with two quick swipes of the knife, freeing it from the branch above.

"You're still choking him!" Vanessa screamed. But it didn't do any good. Every step in Carter's direction only made things worse. Mima seemed like a trapped animal, wild-eyed and unpredictable. This wasn't the same Mima they'd known all during *Raku Nau*, Jane thought. Not anymore.

Something very strange—and very wrong—was going on.

Buzz took a step toward Mima with both hands held out to show he meant no harm. It was all beyond confusing. "Mima, what are you doing? Please, listen!" he said.

"Fah!" she shouted again. *No!*

"Be careful!" Vanessa called out, just as Mima lunged and Buzz jumped back.

"What's going on?" Carter asked. His voice was weak. He seemed too tired to struggle.

"She wants the blood ring," Jane said.

"The *what*?" Carter asked.

"It's what they all came for," Vanessa said. "But Mima! Just listen—"

"She's *not* listening," Buzz said, and tried again. "Mima, please. You can keep him for now. Take the blood ring, whatever you have to do. Just let us talk to Carter."

The words spilled out, whether they were doing

any good or not. Maybe she understood his tone, or his gestures, but it didn't matter. She wasn't letting anyone come close.

Instead, she jerked her head in the direction of the tunnel.

"*Ekka-ko?*" she asked, looking Jane right in the eye. It meant *This way?* But with the *ko* at the end, it was beyond confusing. *Ko* was for enemies. *Ka* was for friends. That much Buzz knew.

Jane was sobbing as she answered. "*Ah-ka-ah,*" she said, meaning *yes*. "But, *ekka-ka,* Mima. *Ekka-KA!* We're your friends! What are you doing?"

Mima's only response was to shove Carter back between the roots of the tree and toward the tunnel entrance. She never let go of the vine even as Carter half slid, half climbed inside. Not that their brother had the energy to run away, from the look of him.

As soon as he'd disappeared into the tunnel, Mima dropped in behind Carter. She didn't try to stop anyone from following. Buzz, Jane, and Vanessa hurried right after them, into the dark, along with several of the other Nukula. Aboveground, one of the other runners had already started working up a fire, hopefully for a torch they could all use.

Meanwhile, Carter was Mima's prisoner, and there was nothing they could do about it. The most they could hope for now was to try to stay as close as possible for the trip back to the eastern shore.

After that, it was anyone's guess.

CHAPTER 11

The return trip through the tunnel was more confusing than anything Buzz had experienced since their shipwreck on Nowhere Island. The small space filled up with bodies and voices in the dark, as half the group felt their way along behind Mima and Carter.

Soon, several of the others showed up with torches to light the way. Buzz had never seen any flint or fire starters on the island. Not like on the survival shows he used to watch. But he *had* seen Nukula of every age start a fire with a vine and a stick about as easily as starting a lawn mower. It was amazing how quickly they were able to light up the tunnel.

Still, the light was their only relief. Everything else was a crazy scramble, competing with the others to get near the front. From the sound of the Nukulas' voices, it seemed as though they were all kissing up to Mima. She was going to wear the blood ring now, after all.

Or maybe they were actually congratulating her. It was hard to tell without understanding the language. But nobody was trying to take Carter from her anymore. It seemed as though *Ohzooka* was officially over.

Soon, the return trip turned into a run, and it got even harder to keep up. All Buzz, Jane, and Vanessa could do was shout to their brother from a distance. There was no time for making a new plan, no time for anything but trying to stay with the group.

"Carter, are you okay?" Buzz called out.

"I'm . . . okay!" Carter called back. But he didn't *sound* okay. He sounded like the running was all he could manage. After that, Buzz and the girls stopped trying to get him to talk. It was awful, not being able to help him or even hear his voice.

Fortunately, the run back was quick. Sooner than Buzz would have thought possible, they reached the ladder below the guard hut near the encampment. Mima pushed Carter up first and went right behind him, still holding the vine like a leash. Everyone else pushed and jostled to be the next ones out. The group streamed up through the hole in the ground, with Buzz and Vanessa somewhere in the middle.

As soon as Buzz was outside, he turned back to look for Jane. He'd lost her in the shuffle to get out.

"Buzz! Vanessa! Over here!" Jane yelled.

He turned again and looked up the trail toward the main clearing. Jane was there, waving them on. She'd already squeezed through ahead of them.

"Why am I even surprised?" he asked as they hurried after her. Jane knew how to use her size as an advantage, that was for sure. She could slip through practically anything unnoticed.

"What do we do now?" she asked as they all continued up the trail.

"What I want to know is what Mima's thinking," Vanessa said. "I don't get it."

"You don't?" Jane asked. "She's making herself a leader in the tribe, that's what."

"But she wouldn't even have a *seccu* if it wasn't for Carter!" Vanessa said.

"I'm not excusing it, I'm just explaining," Jane said. "At least it's her and not someone else."

"It sure sounds like you're excusing it," Vanessa said.

"Shut up, you guys," Buzz said. It was nearly impossible not to lose patience, but they couldn't afford that right now. The only solution was to keep their eyes open and see what they could make out of whatever happened next.

The drums started up as Mima led the procession out of the woods and into the clearing, dragging Carter along beside her. Vanessa watched from several yards back while he stumbled along, still trying to keep pace.

The feast had begun without them. The roasting boar from before now lay, half-carved, on a stone pile, keeping warm by the flames. People sat in groups, spread out around several smaller blazes in the clearing.

Laki alone sat by the main fire, nearest the meat. He had a leaf bundle open on his knee, feeding himself with his hands, when he looked up and saw them coming.

People jumped to their feet and came closer as Mima brought Carter straight to the chief. Vanessa felt Jane's fingers intertwine with her own. Buzz stood close on the other side. There was no sign of Ani so far, and they watched, waiting to see what would happen.

Laki stayed cross-legged on the ground as Mima pushed Carter down to kneel next to him. She didn't say anything at all. She only reached over to cut the loop from Carter's neck, as though she were dropping him off for Laki.

But Laki stopped her with a hand on her arm. He said something to Mima that Vanessa couldn't hear, and then handed her something. It dropped into her palm and he closed her fingers around it.

The blood ring. That's what it had to be, Vanessa

thought. But Laki had made so little deal out of it. Something seemed off. Maybe it had to do with how the tribe had reacted when he took the ring from Chizo in the first place. Or how Laki had been eating alone when they'd come back.

Whatever was going on, there was a definite feeling in the air that Laki no longer enjoyed the love and support of the Nukula as he had just a few days earlier. Even his face looked different—drawn, and sad, to Vanessa's eyes.

Whatever it was, Mima didn't hesitate. She slipped the ring onto her own little finger while Laki continued to address her. He seemed to be giving some kind of instructions, because Mima picked up the vine next and pulled Carter back onto his feet.

Laki motioned toward the far end of the clearing, beyond the light of the fires.

"What do you think he's saying?" Jane asked at Vanessa's side. Vanessa shook her head. Even with everything that had happened, it felt like some kind of bad dream now. As horrible as the last few weeks had been, they'd always stayed in charge of their own fate. Now, it was as though everything they'd fought for was being taken away from them, in a whole new way.

A hand landed on her shoulder, and she flinched. It was Ani. The sight of his face flooded her with relief, and she threw her arms around him.

"Ani! What's happening? Please, tell us!" Vanessa said. "Where is Carter going?"

"He will be bound and held for the night," Ani said. "When the tribe has gone in the morning, the guards will let him out, and he will remain here."

"Carter!" Jane shouted.

This was exactly what they'd been afraid of. It was all coming so fast.

"When your brother ran off this afternoon, he forfeited his right to return to the village," Ani said.

"What do you mean, they're holding him?" Vanessa asked. "Where? How?"

"The guards have prepared a sand pit," Ani said. "They will not hurt him. He will receive food and water. He will be kept there only through the night. But then you will have to say your good-byes."

"No," Vanessa said. There was no question to it. Just—*no*.

"We're not letting him go in there," Buzz said.

Ani looked at them gravely. "I promise you that you have no choice," he said.

"I'll go with him," Vanessa said. "Buzz and Jane, you stay."

"No way!" Jane said.

"That's not going to happen," Buzz said. "You said it yourself, Vanessa. We're not getting separated again. Not ever."

"It does not matter," Ani said. "You three are wearers of the *seccu*. It is not done this way."

"Fine," Vanessa said. She reached up, untied the leather cord around her neck, and held out the stone. "Take it."

She pushed the *seccu* into Ani's hand, then turned toward Laki.

"We're staying wherever our brother is staying," Vanessa said. Her gaze traveled from Laki, to Ani, to the rest of the tribe as Ani translated quietly for the chief. Everyone was watching. "You can try to stop us, but it isn't going to work. I don't care what happens anymore. We're not . . . splitting . . . up."

Her heart was racing, but she wasn't scared. It didn't feel *brave*, either. It was more about doing the only thing she knew to do.

"This is a mistake," Ani said.

"If it is, then we're all making it together," Buzz said. He and Jane had already taken off their own *seccu* as well. All three of them walked over to stand with Carter.

"You guys," Carter mumbled out. "Don't—"

"Shut up," Vanessa said. "We're staying wherever you are."

"*Ozo etta mi shinolaka*," Mima said. Several people laughed nervously.

Vanessa looked into Mima's eyes, searching for some kind of understanding. Mima only stared back, as unblinking as a stone.

"What did she say?" Jane asked.

"She said, 'Blood runs deep,'" Ani answered. "It means the four of you are a family to the end."

"Yeah," Vanessa said, putting out her hands to be tied. "She's right about that."

CHAPTER 12

The pit had been dug during *Ohzooka*. It was the same size and shape as the one on the western beach, where Vanessa had been trapped the first day. Jane looked down inside, but there was nothing to see, just a flat bottom and sand walls that gave way to dirt lower down. It was definitely too far to jump in or climb out.

The pit sat at the far edge of the main clearing, in the direction of *Trehila* and the canoes. Two guards stuck tall torches in the ground all around it and lit them as Carter, Jane, Vanessa, and Buzz were lowered in, one by one, with a vine rope.

As soon as Jane hit the bottom next to Carter, she threw her arms around him.

"I'm so sorry!" she said.

"What are you sorry for?" he asked.

"You must have been so scared on your own!" she said. "At least the three of us have been together."

"I'm okay," Carter said, playing it off the way he always did. But Jane could tell from the tightness in his voice that he felt otherwise. He blamed himself for all of this. If it hadn't been for Carter's sacrifice at the end of *Raku Nau*, they could have been gone by now.

But none of that was worth saying out loud, Jane thought. It was behind them. And the truth was, she might have done the same thing.

"Betzo!" someone said.

Jane turned and saw it was Mima. She'd come down into the pit and was holding more of the thin vines they'd used during the marking ceremony.

Ani stood at the top, along with Laki and several others. Everyone watched from above as Mima continued what seemed to be her job here. She'd captured Carter, and now she would bind all of them for the night.

"You must all sit and have your hands tied," Ani told them.

"What for?" Buzz said. "It's not like we can climb out."

Jane didn't even hear the answer. She was staring at Mima, trying to get her to look back. Mima only kept her eyes down and wrapped Jane's wrist with the vine, then tied it off. The whole thing was so confusing, she didn't even know where to start. Mima had so quickly become a friend, even like a family member to them. This new change was just as sudden, but twice as perplexing.

"Mima?" she said, more than once. But she never got an answer. She never even got a glance. Jane felt a lump in her throat, but her eyes stayed dry. There were simply no more tears to give.

Soon, they were all sitting with their hands tied and their backs propped against the dirt walls. Mima used the vine to walk herself up and out of the pit, then pulled it up behind her. Not once did she look back.

The next surprise came in the form of food and water. The guards dropped down four leaf bundles and two waterskins to share. It was awkward to eat with their hands tied in front of them, but nobody worried about that. There was no conversation, either. After forty-eight hours of starving, there was nothing they needed as much as this.

Just the smell, much less the taste, of the meat and the stringy vegetables in the leaf packet was like a miracle. At home, it all would have tasted like nothing, Jane thought. They probably would have thrown the food away. But here, the idea of throwing away *anything* to eat was inconceivable.

It was amazing what even a little food could do. Carter, especially, seemed to wake up from the trance they'd found him in. It was like watching him come back to life. Jane could have drunk gallons more water than they'd been given, too. Even so, she felt stronger than she had in days.

And then, finally, the conversation began.

There were questions first. Lots of questions. Carter listened as they explained what had happened without him, and how *Ohzooka* had been called after his escape.

Then he told them about his own strange turn with Chizo. It had been Chizo himself who had pointed the way for Carter to run.

"Maybe he was hoping you'd get lost in the jungle," Buzz said.

"Or worse," Vanessa said.

"I don't know," Carter told them, looking up. "It was weird. I could have really taken him out in that fight, and I didn't. I think he was paying me back."

"Yeah, well . . ." Vanessa said, and held up her bound wrists. "I guess it *almost* worked. Thanks for nothing, Mima."

"I can't believe she'd do this," Jane said.

"Don't say that," Carter told her. He looked up again, Jane noticed, but there was nothing to see. Just the starry sky and the back of one of the guards.

"Why not?" Vanessa asked. "Listen, I get it. She had to do what she had to do. But meanwhile . . . well, never mind."

Vanessa sat back again and shut her mouth.

"You can say it," Jane told her. "We're stuck. They're going to try and take us away from Carter in the morning. And there's nothing we can do about it now."

"Did Mima really need the blood ring that badly?" Buzz asked. "She already had the *seccu*."

"Listen," Carter said. "We wouldn't turn on each other, would we? Mima wouldn't do that to us, either."

"What are you talking about?" Buzz shot back. "She just did!"

"Omigosh, do you still *like* her?" Vanessa asked. "What's wrong with you? This is about way more than a crush, Carter."

Carter didn't take the bait. He kept his voice low. "I'm just saying, we're going to be okay," he told them.

"How can you say that?" Buzz asked.

"And why do you keep looking up?" Jane added.

When she looked for herself, the guard had stepped away from the edge of the pit. She could hear him talking to the other one, nearby.

Carter glanced up once more. Then he leaned forward and rolled to the side, showing them the dirt wall behind his back. It was too dark to see much in the pit, but Jane could tell something was there. It had been shoved into the soft earth, she saw, just before Carter moved back into place.

When she looked up again, the guard was there, staring down at them.

"What was that?" she asked Carter in a whisper.

Carter looked around at each of them in turn. "This is what I've been trying to tell you," he said quietly. "Right after Mima tied me up, she gave me her knife."

Carter laughed for the first time since he could remember. The wide eyes on all three of his siblings were clear, even in the dark pit.

"I knew it!" Jane said. "I knew she couldn't just turn her back on us."

"Why didn't you say something?" Vanessa asked.

"I just did," Carter said.

"But what does it mean?" Jane asked. "What are we supposed to do with it?"

"It's not like we're going to . . . stab anyone," Vanessa said.

"And even if we cut ourselves free, how do we get out? And past the guards?" Buzz asked.

It was still strange, speaking out loud for anyone to hear. But the guard didn't even turn around.

"I don't know," Carter said. "But I knew something had to be up."

"She didn't have any choice!" Jane said. He could tell how relieved she was. All of them loved Mima, but for Jane, it had seemed especially hard to see her turn on them. "She had to take Carter, or someone else would have."

"And she had to be convincing," Carter said. "Otherwise, she couldn't . . ."

He trailed off, not sure what to say.

"She couldn't what?" Jane asked.

"I don't know," he said. "But this isn't over."

"Maybe we're supposed to use the knife for digging," Buzz said.

"Dig where?" Vanessa asked.

There was no answer for that one. Carter didn't know the encampment as well as the others, but he'd seen enough to know there was nowhere to go from this level.

"She probably wasn't planning on all four of us being down here," Buzz said.

"That's my fault," Vanessa answered. She sounded upset all over again.

"No," Carter said. "If it's anyone's fault, you guys—"

"It's nobody's fault!" Jane interrupted. "Okay? And even if it were, so what? None of that changes anything now. Not anymore."

"Well, I hope Mima has a *really* good idea," Vanessa said.

"She does," Carter said.

"How can you be so sure?" Buzz asked.

Carter didn't have to think about his answer. Somehow, everything they'd been through—even the day they'd just had—was so impossible, it made anything seem just a little more possible.

"Because she's amazing," he said. "She's the most

amazing person I've ever met. And it's not because I *like* her, okay?"

"Yeah, right," Vanessa said, giving her I'm-older-and-I-know-better look. "Not *just* because you like her, anyway."

"Whatever," Carter said. "I also trust her. And so should you. Because if you ask me, this night's just getting started."

CHAPTER 13

Buzz woke up to the smell of smoke.

After everything that had happened, he never thought for a second he'd fall asleep in that pit. But the hours had worn on, and the long day had caught up to him. Somewhere along the way, each of them had dropped off.

Now he was sitting up again, wide awake.

"Do you hear that?" Jane asked.

People were shouting. Buzz could hear the crackle of burning wood, too, far louder than any single campfire. When he looked up, a glowing light showed from the direction of the main clearing.

"Something's wrong—" Vanessa started to say, but she was cut off by the crashing sound of a burning limb hitting the ground.

"That was a branch," Buzz said. "A big one."

"It's the trees," Jane said. "It sounds like they're on fire."

Carter was the first onto his feet. "This is it!" he said. Already, he had Mima's knife clasped between his bound hands.

The guards were nowhere Buzz could see. From the sound of all the voices, it made sense they would have gone to help. There was no knowing for sure.

"Buzz, here!" Carter said. "Let me cut you free."

Buzz held out his hands, and Carter sawed at the vines around his wrists.

"Careful!" Buzz said.

"Just stay still," he said. It wasn't long before the cordage split and popped open. Buzz shook his fingers and rubbed at his wrists to get the circulation back.

"Now me," Carter said.

It didn't take long to cut everyone loose. Even if

they were caught, Buzz thought, there wasn't much the guards could do but retie them. Still, his heart was going like he'd just sprinted a mile. Because if they *didn't* get caught . . .

The possibilities stretched all the way to Chicago.

"I'll go up first," Vanessa said.

There was no discussion. Carter and Buzz each took a leg and boosted Vanessa as high as they could. Vanessa kept her body stiff. Even now, after weeks of struggling to survive, her years of gymnastics showed. In a moment, she had her hands on the edge of the pit. But as she grabbed on, the sandy edge crumbled away, faster than she could climb out.

Sand fell into Buzz's eyes and mouth. He spit and shook his head, trying to see without letting go. They still had to get Vanessa out.

"Can you get me any higher?" she asked.

"One, two, three—*push!*" Carter said.

Buzz heaved as hard as he could. He had her by the bottom of the foot now. Carter, too. She rose another several inches, wavered, and nearly tipped over. But in the next second, Vanessa was pushing off from their hands and kicking her way up the last few feet to keep from sliding back in.

"Is anyone around?" Buzz asked.

"Hang on," Vanessa said. And then, "This fire's huge, you guys! Everyone's over there—"

"Find something to get us out!" Carter said. "Hurry!"

"It's right here," Vanessa answered. One end of the vine rope tumbled into the pit. "Jane, you come first! You're the lightest. Then we can get the guys out."

Jane was up and out a few seconds later. Then Carter, then Buzz.

As Buzz came onto flat ground again, the scene in front of him was like something from a movie. The trees at the opposite end of the encampment were all one huge curtain of fire now. People were running in and out of the light, bringing water from the beach. Others were throwing sand, or chopping away what they could. There were shouts everywhere. It was chaos.

Which was maybe the whole idea.

"This is our chance!" Jane said. "We need to get to Ani's canoe, and someone needs to open that screen."

"Where?" Carter asked, looking around.

It took a second for Buzz to remember Carter had not been this way before.

"There!" Buzz said, pointing toward the trail, and they all sprinted straight for it.

The screen they were headed toward was huge, Vanessa knew. It was going to take a miracle to open it. But she kept her thoughts to herself. They'd do what they could when they got there.

Meanwhile, she watched her footing as they moved along the dark path. The fire behind them was enough to penetrate the woods with a small amount of light, but not much.

"I'll get the boat ready when we get there," Jane said. "Carter, give me the knife. I can cut it loose while you three work on the screen. Then I'll meet you downstream."

"We can't split up!" Vanessa said. "Are you crazy?"

"Is there anything about this that *isn't* crazy?" Jane asked.

"She's right, Nessa," Buzz said. "We don't have time to mess around."

They'd just arrived at the canoes. A dozen or more of them bobbed and shifted together, where they were tethered in the fast-moving water. The screen was another fifty yards or more off to their right, where the channel flowed into the ocean.

"That boat?" Jane asked. She pointed to Ani's outrigger, on the downstream side of all the others.

"That's it," Buzz said.

It had been the last one in, which meant it would be easy to get it away. Maybe Ani had even planned it like that.

Still, there had been no time to talk about what it would mean to get back onto the open ocean. Ani had promised coconuts and water. Hopefully, those were already on board. Whatever else Jane could pull together right now would have to be enough.

"Do what you can," Vanessa told her. "Cut some fronds. We can use them for shade. And grab anything else you can find. But don't cut the boat loose until we're back."

"It'll be faster if I cut it when I'm ready and meet you down there," Jane said.

"The current's too tricky," Vanessa said. "You'll get washed right past us if we're not careful."

Jane didn't argue. The one thing they didn't have right now was time. Without another word, Vanessa turned downstream with Buzz and Carter to head for the enormous gate at the far end of the channel.

"We'll see you in a minute," she called back, and kept on moving.

Jane worked with what little light she had from the fires. She ran up and down the bank, cutting every big leaf and frond she could reach, then piling them into Ani's canoe. There was no time to pick and choose. They could be caught by the elders or the guards at any second.

She could see some waterskins were already in the boat, and two big bunches of coconuts, still on the stem. It didn't look like much. They'd have to ration.

But first, and most of all, they had to get away.

After three trips up and down the bank, she turned again—and stopped short. Someone was coming up the trail. She could see a torch but nothing else.

Jane stepped back and dropped into Ani's canoe. Had she been seen? Was it all over, just like that? Lying flat, she stayed out of sight, listening for whoever it was.

There were footsteps. And then a voice.

"Car-tare? Jane?"

Mima's voice.

"Buzz? Ba-nessa?" she said.

Jane's breath was fast and shaky. There was no knowing anything for sure right now, but she took the risk and sat up.

"Mima?" she said.

"Jane!" she said. *"Betta a tikka, Car-tare? Buzz betto, Ba-nessa?"*

Jane shot out of the canoe and up the bank. Mima went stiff when Jane tried to hug her, but it wasn't like before when she'd captured Carter. That was just the way Mima was. She busied herself instead, scraping her torch against the ground to put it out.

She was probably trying to avoid being seen, now that they'd found each other.

It was all making sense. And Mima was as strong as any of them. Stronger, in fact. She'd be able to help get the screen open.

"Over there!" Jane said, pointing downstream. "*Ekka-ka!* Go and help them, please! *Ekka-ka?*"

"*Ekka-ka,*" Mima said.

Even now, it was a relief to hear the *ka*—for *friends.* Mima had been so full of anger before. Or at least, she'd been acting like it for the tribe.

She pressed a bundle of some kind into Jane's hands. Then she said something else in Nukula and disappeared downstream to go help the others.

The bundle was probably more supplies, Jane thought. It was tied up with a vine, and she dropped it into the canoe. Her time was better spent gathering fronds right now. They'd sort everything else out later.

It was only after Mima had moved on that Jane realized who had probably started this whole fire. And why.

Thank you, Mima. Thank you, thank you.
Forever.

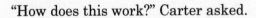

"How does this work?" Carter asked.

They'd told him about the bamboo-and-foliage gate, but seeing it was different. He'd imagined something smaller. This thing was as tall as a house.

"It slides open," Vanessa said. "At least, it did when they had a whole bunch of people on both sides of it."

"All right. We've got this," Carter said, though it was hard to know for sure. "Let's go. I want to get back to Jane."

"Wait!" Buzz said. He looked upstream. "Someone's coming."

"Let's go then! Hurry!" Carter said. He already had his hands on the bamboo frame.

"Car-tare!"

Mima's voice stopped him. She was there now, not much more than a shadow. But even the shadow moved just like her.

"Over here!" Vanessa said. She motioned for Mima, trying to show what they wanted to do.

Carter could tell she understood right away—not just what had to happen, but the need to keep moving. She had her hands on the frame next to him before Vanessa and Buzz were even in position.

"So, do we just—" Vanessa started to say.

"PULL!" Carter said. He bore down with his feet in the dirt as hard as he could. Then he locked his fingers around the fat piece of bamboo and heaved with the others.

Amazingly, the gate moved on the first pull. There was a groove in the ground, and the whole thing slid several feet before they lost momentum.

Carter's heart surged.

"Again!" he said.

"Etto farka!" Mima said. *Farka* was the word for *storm*. And they were fighting like one right now.

They heaved a second time. The frame seemed to stick in the ground, but then gave way all at once. Carter fell back, jumped up, and grabbed on again.

"Keep going!" he said, and they did.

The screen dragged toward them like the wall of a house moving through the dirt. Carter managed a step back. Then another.

"It's working!" he said.

All at once, the whole thing gave a hard jerk as the opposite side of the screen left the far bank of the channel. The frame suddenly rose in his hands, pulling him right off the ground while the other side dropped toward the water.

"No, no, no!" Vanessa yelled.

It was too heavy. There was no time to switch tactics. The far corner of the frame crashed down, wedging itself into the channel at a crazy angle.

Carter still hadn't let go. He hung five or six feet above the water now, and quickly pulled himself up to sit on the frame itself. The current rushed by underneath him.

"What now?" Buzz asked.

"Actually . . ." Carter said.

It was hard to gauge in the dark, but it looked very much like there was enough room on this side of the channel for a canoe to slip under the tilted gate.

"We can still do this!" he said—just before several voices came up from the woods.

Carter looked in that direction and saw the flame of a torch. Then another. Someone was coming their way.

They'd been spotted.

CHAPTER 14

Buzz saw the torches, and his heart dropped.

"We've got to go. Like, right now," he told Vanessa. She was farther down the bank and hadn't seen anyone coming yet.

"All right, let's go!" she said, and pointed upstream. "Carter! This way!"

"No, I mean, there's no time for that," Buzz said.

"He's right," Carter said, and yelled up the channel. "*Jane!* Change of plans. We have to go! Cut the boat loose!"

There was a tense pause. Not a silence, though. The fire and the chaos in camp filled the air with sound and light. So did the torch carriers, coming closer through the woods.

"Now?" Jane's voice came back.

"Yes!" Carter yelled. "Bring the canoe! There's no time to explain!"

"What about the current?" Vanessa asked. "She's going to wash right past us!"

"Not if we catch her," Carter said. "Everyone spread out. Buzz, grab one of those pieces of bamboo and hold it over the water. We just need to slow her down enough to get in, and then we're gone."

Buzz looked up. Carter was already on the frame of the gate itself, sliding farther out over the channel. The whole thing sat cockeyed, with the far corner stuck in the water. The other corner, nearest them, was at least four feet above the channel. That's where the canoe could pass. But first they'd have to slow the boat enough to get in.

"Nessa!" Buzz said. "Up there! Next to Carter." Vanessa was the tallest. She was the gymnast, too. "If you hang upside down, you'll be able to reach anything that passes by. I'll work from here with Mima."

He bent down and picked up an end of the heaviest bamboo he could spot. Several pieces had been used as braces to keep the screen in place when it was closed. He held it with both arms and turned clumsily to pivot it over the water, like another kind of gate. If nothing else, it would help slow the boat while Vanessa and Carter worked from above.

"Mima, help me with this!" he said. He was pointing to the bamboo and then upstream, desperate to get his meaning across. Everyone else was better at communicating with her. But she'd gotten pretty good at understanding them, too. "Jane's coming!" he said.

Mima came and stood with him on the bank, securing the pole together from one end. Even she didn't try wading into the current. There would be no keeping their footing that way. They'd have a better chance of giving Jane a barrier to crash into by holding it steady from where they were.

"JANE!" Carter yelled again. "Have you got it? Can you do this?"

More Nukula shouts filled the air. Some of them

were closer than ever. In the noise, Buzz couldn't even tell if Jane had answered.

But it was too late to do anything else. Now they had to wait and hope she showed up with the boat soon.

Really soon.

Jane looked downstream. All she could see was the fast current running off into the dark. The screen was too far to make out, but she could hear the others shouting for her. And the voices in the woods, too. They all blended together.

Her hands shook as she stood up in the boat. She leaned out as far as she could and pressed the edge of the stone knife into the vine tether that held the canoe in place.

This was it. As soon as she sawed through the vine, they were going to be thrown into a whole new kind of unknown. They were just as unprepared for this as they'd been for Nowhere Island, for Shadow Island, for all of it. The realization hit like a heavy weight in the bottom of her stomach.

What were they thinking? How were they possibly going to survive out there, maybe for days—or even weeks? They were going to need so much more than the few supplies they had. Even something like the vine rope in her hand could be a lifesaver out on the open ocean. In fact—

Jane didn't think—she moved. She jumped out of the canoe and ran up the bank to where the vine was tied off to a tree. If she could cut it from this end, that would be at least fifteen feet of rope they could bring with them.

She grabbed the vine near the tree trunk and spiraled her hand around it, until it was tight on her wrist. Then she gripped it hard and reached with the other hand to cut the whole thing free.

"Jane!" Vanessa called. "Where are you?"

"Here I come!" she said. "Get ready!"

"We got you!" Carter yelled. "Don't worry!"

Too late, Jane thought.

Here went everything. She sawed into the vine several times with the edge of the blade. The vine tore, but held. She sawed even harder—once, twice, three times—and then it popped.

The outrigger's response was immediate. It turned on the current, away from the other boats, and started downstream. Jane ran and then stumbled down the bank to catch up. She threw the knife into the canoe and dove to get inside, a fraction too late. Instead, she hit the water. The rope snapped tight on her wrist and yanked her downstream, towing her behind the canoe toward the others.

Everything was a dark blur of movement and water. Jane reached and pulled herself higher on the vine as it continued along the channel. It was like climbing sideways toward the boat, hand over hand, working against the water, the momentum, all of it.

With the next pull, she felt something solid. It was the side of the boat. She reached up again, grabbed on, and heaved herself inside. The whole thing nearly tipped over as she did, just before she landed on her back in the well of the canoe.

"JANE! NOW!" Vanessa's voice came right away.

Jane sprang back up and looked around. The enormous screen was straight ahead and approaching fast. The whole thing was crooked now, half in the water and half out. She saw the others, too. Carter and Vanessa hung off the gate itself, with Buzz and Mima holding something out from the shore. It was a big piece of bamboo. She recognized it just as the canoe crashed into it, knocking the pole right out of Buzz's and Mima's hands.

"NO!" Buzz yelled. "Vanessa! Get her!"

The canoe shimmied on the water and cut toward the bank. Vanessa was straight ahead now. Carter was off to the side, too far to reach.

Vanessa dropped even lower to hang by her knees. Jane stood up to get to her, but the boat was too unsteady and she fell right back down again.

"Buzz, get in the boat!" Carter yelled.

"I can't!" he said. "It's too far! This was a mistake!"

"I've got her!" Vanessa screamed. "Get up, Jane! Give me your hand!"

Jane popped back up in the wobbling canoe and reached as high as she could for Vanessa's grasp.

Vanessa squeezed the bamboo gate tightly with her

legs. Her knees were either going to hold, or they weren't. There was no time to change position.

She stretched her hands down toward Jane's as her little sister and the canoe rushed under her. Their fingers found one another and locked together.

"I've got you!" she said.

Her knuckles strained and cracked from the tight grip. Jane screamed out in pain.

Still, it wasn't going to be enough. Vanessa groaned, digging for the strength to hold on. If she let go to get a better grip, Jane would wash away. But they couldn't stay like this, either.

"CARTER!" she yelled.

"I'm coming!" he said. He was close but not there yet.

Jane had her feet hooked into the canoe's frame now. The current was pulling on it, like gravity toward the ocean.

"Just let go of the boat!" Vanessa said. "Forget about it!"

"No! We can do this!" Jane screamed back. Her eyes were wide with fear, but she wasn't letting go.

"CARTER! NOW!" Vanessa said.

"I'm here!" he said. He flipped down next to her. "Jane, give me your hand!"

Jane turned to look at him. Then she pulled one hand free from Vanessa's grip and reached his way.

"Wait! Don't!" Vanessa shouted, but it was too late. Before Carter could grab her, Jane's other hand slipped free. Vanessa felt their fingers untangle, and she could only watch as Jane fell back once more. The last thing she saw was Jane's head hitting the side of the canoe, hard.

"JANE!" she screamed.

Jane didn't answer.

"JANE!"

Already, the current had carried her past the screen, through the mouth of the channel, and out toward the dark ocean beyond.

CHAPTER 15

Carter jumped from the giant frame down to the bank and ran toward the shore, calling his sister's name as the canoe slipped away.

He didn't get far. Mima was right there, pulling him back before he even reached the beach.

"What are you doing? We have to get her!" he yelled.

"Mima, let him go!" Vanessa said.

"*Fah!*" Mima answered, and pointed straight up instead of out toward the boat. "*Trehila! Trehila!*" she said.

Carter looked up. The trunk of the enormous palm was right over their heads, where it curved like a one-way bridge above the ocean. In the tree's crown, the guard hut sat at the farthest point over the water—and also well ahead of the canoe itself.

"She's right!" Vanessa said. "We'll never swim fast enough to catch up, but if we hurry—"

"We can jump from up there!" Carter said.

There was no time to weigh options. And Mima's instincts had never steered them wrong. They were already moving toward the base of the tree, with Mima in the lead.

"What about Chizo?" Vanessa asked. "We don't know if he's still up there."

"It'll be okay," Carter said.

"How do you know?" Vanessa asked.

The other Nukula had reached the boat depot now. They were starting to make their way downstream. Carter could hear them and see the torches coming closer.

"It'll have to be," he said, and started up the ladder behind Mima.

"And what about the jump?" Buzz said. "That's almost a hundred feet up. We've never done anything like that. Not even close."

"That'll have to be okay, too," Carter said grimly. And he kept on climbing.

Vanessa was twenty feet off the ground before she had to slow down at all. The ladder was lashed to the trunk, and the climbing was easy so far. Now she practically had Carter's heels in her face with every step.

"Go, go, go, go, go!" she said. "We have to hurry!"

"I am!" Carter said.

Mima led the way, and she moved faster than any of them. She quickly put some distance between herself and their group, while Vanessa, Carter, and Buzz worked to keep up.

Gradually, the tree curved out toward the water. It grew at an impossible angle, as if it were too huge and proud ever to go down.

As they passed the treetops of the forest around them, the trunk thinned, and the climbing got harder. Vanessa kept her body pressed close to the ladder, and to the tree itself. It was turning into less of a climb and more of a pull as she dragged herself along.

The vines of the ladder started to get in the way, too. Vanessa's foot caught in one of the rungs, and she lurched out over the side of the trunk.

Suddenly, she was looking straight down. They were already far higher than she had even realized. The ocean below was just a flat expanse of black, except near the shore, where the fires lit up the water.

"There she is!" Vanessa said as she spotted the canoe.

Jane was on her back, and barely stirring. The canoe had slowed, but it wasn't stopping and it wasn't changing direction. Every second took it farther away from the island.

"Jane!" she yelled. "Jane! Up here!"

"Nessa?" Jane called out. Just the sound of her weak voice through the night air was a relief. At least Jane was conscious.

"We're coming! Just stay put!" Vanessa yelled back. The only thing to do now was to keep climbing.

Slowly—horribly slowly—they progressed toward the top. The tree continued to curve until it had all but flattened out near the end, where the guard hut waited.

Vanessa stayed low, pulling herself along, bumping over the vine rungs and the rough bark. The trunk was barely as wide as her body now, and a fall felt much more likely. All it would take was one more slip like the last one.

"Buzz? Are you okay?" she called back, without looking.

"Unh," was all Buzz answered. It was a yes, but even words were too much of an effort right now.

"Almost there!" Carter called out.

Vanessa risked a quick glance ahead. Maybe thirty feet in front of her, the guard hut stood against a backdrop of *Trehila*'s enormous fronds. Mima was nearly to it. Carter was right behind her.

And there on the platform stood Chizo, watching them approach.

CHAPTER 16

Carter wished he was ahead of Mima. But at least he was ahead of Vanessa and Buzz. If one of the three of them was going to risk facing Chizo first, it was going to be him.

Chizo held a spear out to keep Mima from leaving the ladder or standing up on the hut's platform. She stayed low, clinging to the trunk the same way Carter was doing. A hundred feet of air beneath him looked like twice as much as it had from the ground. His heart thudded right into the wood with a fast, steady rhythm.

Mima stayed where she was. The pointed end of

Chizo's weapon was nearly between her eyes. She said something in Nukula, but Chizo didn't move or speak in return.

Carter stole another look straight down. Jane and the canoe were almost directly under them now, and still drifting. She was about to pass them by.

"There's no time!" he said between clenched teeth. And there wasn't. But there also wasn't anything he could do to make this go faster. He could only watch and wait to see what happened.

Mima slowly let go of the ladder to reach up toward Chizo with one hand. "Mima, NO!" Carter screamed. All it would take from Chizo now was one push, and she'd be gone. What was she thinking?

Chizo reached out, but his spear was down. His hand closed around Mima's wrist, and he bent closer to look at something on her hand. That's what it seemed like, anyway. None of it was making any sense.

"It's the blood ring!" Vanessa yelled from behind. "She's showing it to him! But Mima! Please hurry! Jane's drifting away!"

"Mima!" Carter called out again.

"Ah-ka-ah!" she answered. Already she was moving onto the platform as Chizo made way.

Carter pressed his hands onto either side of the trunk and dragged himself the last several feet as fast as he could. Chizo did nothing to stop him as he stood up on the platform, but he moved in close. His face practically pressed into Carter's, as close as his spear had been to Mima a moment ago.

Carter held his breath. What was this?

When Chizo reached up to touch his shoulder, Carter braced himself. It seemed as though Chizo was about to throw him off the platform. If he did, it would at least be enough warning for Buzz and Vanessa to turn back.

Instead, Chizo only moved him aside. He reached out and helped Vanessa take the last step onto the platform. Then Vanessa did the same for Buzz.

It seemed as though maybe a debt had been paid. Carter's thoughts went back to their fight that morning, and the way he'd stepped away from Chizo instead of finishing him like he could have. Or maybe this had something to do with the blood ring. Maybe

Mima had promised Chizo something—or even threatened him with her new authority. Whatever had happened, there was no time to figure it out.

"Where is she?" Vanessa asked, crossing to the far side of the platform. Mima was already there, looking straight down and calling Jane's name.

Carter and Buzz came right behind. The whole platform was no more than fifteen feet across, with a roof on one side and a natural covering of fronds on the other. It was also open to the water below.

"There!" Vanessa said.

Carter saw Jane, waiting in the canoe and looking up at them. The fires on the shore provided just enough light to see by. But the drop was impossible.

The idea of making this jump seemed crazy, Carter thought. It was beyond anything they'd ever done, or even imagined having to do. But meanwhile, Jane was drifting farther and farther from the island. Literally every second counted right now.

Which is what told Carter he needed to do this.

He *would* do it.

They all would.

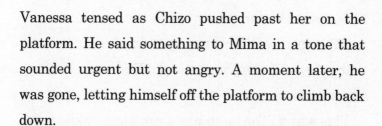

Vanessa tensed as Chizo pushed past her on the platform. He said something to Mima in a tone that sounded urgent but not angry. A moment later, he was gone, letting himself off the platform to climb back down.

Several of the other Nukula had reached the base of *Trehila* by now. Maybe Chizo was going to meet them. Or even block them from climbing. There was no knowing, but she was grateful for whatever he could do.

Now it was time to go. She turned to Mima and looked into her eyes. In the dark, it was hard to see if there was any emotion there, but probably not. Mima was never one to show what she was feeling.

"Mima . . ." Vanessa said. She wished she had the Nukula words to communicate even a small amount of what she wanted to say. Still, she kept going. "I'm sorry. I shouldn't have doubted you. Thank you so much!"

"Stop talking and keep moving!" Buzz said. He took her by the arm and steered her toward the edge of the platform.

Vanessa refocused on the water below. Jane was still there. She was close enough to reach, but she wouldn't be for long. The current continued to carry her away.

"We can do this," Vanessa told Buzz. She was telling herself, too, she realized. There was no time. Not even for courage.

This was it. The jump was a complete unknown. A bad bet here wasn't just going to hurt them. It could end everything. But all Vanessa had to do was look down once more and see Jane alone in that canoe. Then it didn't feel like a decision at all.

"I'll go first," Carter said.

"No," Vanessa told him.

She caught a glimpse of the resistance in his eyes, just before she turned, took a step off the platform, and pushed away with the other foot, into a free fall.

Buzz followed Vanessa like there was a rope between them, pulling him right off the platform.

He fell.

And fell.

The air rushed out of his lungs. His heartbeat overwhelmed everything else as his vision grayed and blurred. It seemed to go on forever, but was also somehow over in a blink. His brain registered the need to get his feet beneath him—his toes pointed—as he slammed into the ocean with a violent crash that gave way to a cocoon of water in nearly the same moment.

Buzz felt the water but saw nothing, heard nothing. He barely even sensed anything. Did he black out? He didn't know. But suddenly, his head was out of the water again. He was blinking, wondering where he was. And then just as fast, he remembered.

"Buzz!" Vanessa yelled. "This way!"

The canoe was there. He saw it before he saw Vanessa. But then she came into view, too. She was in the water, holding on to the side of the boat and waving him over.

Jane was sitting up high in the canoe with a coil of vine rope on her arm. She had it held out over the water, ready to throw his way like a lifeline.

"Buzz! Catch!" she said. "I'll pull you in!"

CHAPTER 17

arter's emotions were overwhelming. He'd never felt so many things at the same time in his life. And the whole idea of saying good-bye to Mima had just been compressed into a matter of seconds. It was going to be over as fast as that—as if it had never happened.

"Thank you!" he said. There were tears in his eyes, and he threw his arms around Mima. It was something he'd never done before. "You saved our lives. We love you, Mima," he said in her ear. He knew she couldn't understand. But maybe she felt it.

"And I always will," he choked out. "I'll never forget you. Ever."

Mima didn't pull away. Her body was stiff, but she reached up to touch him gently on the arm. Carter hated to let go. Still, the need to leave was everything right now. Even more important than Mima.

"Good-bye," he said, choking out the word as he stepped back.

"Goot-bye," she answered. There was no knowing what would happen to her after this. But now that she had the blood ring, she was probably going to run the tribe one day.

"And thank you," Carter said. *"Ratta,* Mima. *Ratta."*

"Carter!" a voice came from below. It was Vanessa. Her shout cut through everything else. He looked all the way down to the water, where the outrigger had moved far out from shore. Maybe too far. He'd have to swim for it.

"Ratta, Car-tare," Mima said, and pointed the way he had to go. *"Ekka-ka! Betzo, Buzz, Jane, Ba-nessa!"*

He looked at her one more time. He took three big strides back from the edge and lowered his center of gravity like pressing into a starting block. Then Carter pushed off into a sprint that took him across the platform and straight out into the night air.

It was terrifying for Jane, watching each of them jump, and then fall, from the top of *Trehila*. Carter plummeted, then hit the water at a scary angle—and nowhere near close enough to the canoe.

Buzz and Vanessa were already back paddling hard. Jane leaned over the edge and used her hands in the water, for whatever good it did. Finally, the canoe moved closer to Carter. When they came near enough, she threw the rope out and they pulled him in the last several yards.

"Is everyone okay?" he gasped out, even as Jane hugged him tight.

"We will be," she said. She pressed herself against Carter, and they both sank deeper into the boat, without enough energy to move any more than that. Buzz and Vanessa took up the paddles, but the current still had them, too. For the moment, it did most of the work.

Slowly, Jane turned and looked back. On the shore,

she could see nearly all of the Nukula watching from various places. Some were right there at the mouth of the channel. Others stood along the edge of the woods. But nobody was coming closer. Nobody even shouted out. And there was no sign of Laki or Chizo, either.

Then, on the easternmost tip, beyond *Trehila* and the channel itself, Jane spotted Ani. He stood alone as he held up a hand to wave good-bye. And even though all of the big fires were nearly out now, she could just make out his face. She wondered if it was the first time she'd ever seen Ani smile.

Jane, Carter, Vanessa, and Buzz all watched him silently. They'd never be able to thank Ani for everything he'd done. But they'd never forget him, either. And they'd never betray his trust, Jane knew. They'd never tell the secrets of the Nukula to the outside world. It was the least they could do.

Slowly, Jane came onto her knees and held up both hands. Then she curved her knuckles in and knocked them together twice, before Ani returned the gesture.

Be strong.

You, too.

It was all the good-bye they would ever have. She watched him on the shore for as long as she could. Shadow Island was quickly slipping away behind them.

"What's this?" Buzz asked from the other end of the boat.

Finally, Jane tore her eyes away. She turned and sat back next to Carter again, as Buzz held up the tied bundle from before.

"I don't know what it is," Jane answered. "Mima gave it to me."

Buzz yanked the vine off and unrolled the leaf. Something spilled out and fell with a soft clunk onto the floor of the canoe. When he held it up, Jane realized that the package may have been delivered by Mima, but what was inside had come from Ani.

It was the three *seccu* she thought they'd left behind.

CHAPTER 18

The night didn't last long. Whatever time it had been when Mima set the fires, the sky soon lightened from black to something more like deep blue. Eventually, that gave way to an endless long line of yellow, then orange and red, as the sun peered up over the horizon.

For hours, there had been no need for paddling. The same current that brought them to Shadow Island's western shore seemed to be carrying them away from its eastern side.

As the day came on, though, the current gradually slowed to a standstill. By the time the sun was fully up, Shadow Island had long since disappeared behind them, and the ocean stretched to a flat nothingness in every direction.

"Welcome to Benson-Diaz Island," Jane said, breaking what had been an hour or more of silence.

Buzz managed a weak laugh. Jane wasn't wrong about that. The canoe itself was everything they had now, like their family's own tiny island. The only reason he wasn't panicking completely was because of the other three in the boat with him.

They had an unspoken pact now. A family deal. Nobody did anything to make this harder for anyone else. They'd made it this far together. They'd find their way home together, too.

Or they'd figure something else out.

All four of them, no matter what.

No words necessary.

Carter slept and woke in short bursts. Like the others, he kept himself covered with the fronds they'd brought, keeping at least partially out of the sun.

When his eyes opened this time, he looked straight up, scanning the blue cloudless sky. Mom and Dad were out there somewhere. That much was for sure. Their parents had searched nonstop while the kids were on Nowhere Island. And that meant they were searching nonstop right now.

Carter knew from the maps they'd had on Uncle Dexter's boat (was it really only three weeks ago?) that the stretch of ocean around them was as big as half the United States. It wasn't impossible to be spotted in a place like this, but unless they got very lucky, they were going to be in for a long wait.

Maybe a *very* long one.

"What do we do if we see land?" Jane asked.

"I say we go to it, at least just to look around," Carter said.

"I agree," Buzz said. "It's a chance to get more supplies, maybe even more water."

"That's *if* we see land," Vanessa said. Because they all knew that wasn't going to happen any time soon. From where Carter sat, looking around in every direction, there was nothing to see at all.

Much less anything to move toward.

Vanessa peeked out over the edge of the boat. The only way to know if they were moving was to look down at the water. Gauging their progress by the vast sky was impossible. But the position of the sun told her it was getting on toward late afternoon. They'd been drifting for at least twelve hours now. Maybe more.

At least the water was calm, she thought, and pulled the frond back over her head.

"Um . . ." Jane said from the other end of the boat. "You guys? What's that?"

Vanessa bolted up. Jane and Carter threw off their sunshades, too, and looked around.

Jane was pointing to the southwest.

"Is it a tree? Or a log?" Buzz said. "Or . . . something else?"

Vanessa squinted in that direction. She saw what he meant, but it took a minute before she could pick out any details. Then her heart jumped. The thing was much farther off than she'd thought at first—which meant it was way bigger than just a log.

"I think it's land!" she said.

"It's an island!" Jane said.

"Actually . . ." Carter came onto his knees, staring in the same direction. "It's more than one island. There's a whole chain of them."

He'd barely said it before he was back down again, paddle in hand. Vanessa picked up the other one, and they bent to it, moving the canoe over the glassy water toward their new find. It was too early to say just how good this news might be. But it had already become clear that if they were going to be out here for a long time, they were going to need more supplies than they had in the boat.

"I hope there's water," Vanessa said.

"What'll we carry it in?" Jane asked.

"We'll figure it out," Buzz said. "First, we just need to . . ."

Vanessa dipped her paddle into the water, pulling as hard as she could. Carter paddled behind her in perfect sync. They were already picking up speed.

"We just need to what?" Jane asked Buzz. But he didn't answer. Instead, the boat rocked hard and nearly tipped as he repositioned himself behind Vanessa.

"Buzz, be careful!" Carter shouted. "And sit down! The last thing we need right now is—"

"Turn around," Buzz said.

"What?" Carter asked.

"Turn around," Buzz repeated. His voice was low, but urgent. Strangely urgent.

"What is it?" Vanessa asked. She twisted around to look at him, and he was staring in the opposite direction of the islands now. The far eastern sky had gone turquoise in the late-afternoon light. Other than that, Vanessa couldn't see anything.

"What are you looking at?" Jane asked.

"That!" Buzz said, pointing.

Vanessa looked again. She squinted. And then she saw the plane.

"Carter, stop paddling!" she said. "Look!"

It couldn't have been tinier. The plane was barely a speck on the horizon. It made no sound at all—or, at least, didn't appear to. It was too far off for that. But it was headed in their direction.

"Is that them?" Jane asked. "Is it . . . I mean, could it be . . ."

Buzz finished the question for her. "Mom and Dad?" he asked.

And the answer was—possibly. Very, very possibly.

Either way, it was *someone.*

This was incredible. Vanessa glanced back at the small island chain. She wasn't even sure why. Then she locked her eyes on the plane again. Carter, Jane, and Buzz were already waving and shouting.

"HEY! HEY!"

"OVER HERE!"

"HELP!"

The plane was too far off to have spotted them yet. But Vanessa quickly joined in. There was no sitting still and keeping quiet now, even if she wanted to. From the direction the plane was headed, there would be no chance for it to miss them. One way or another, something huge was about to happen.

"THIS WAY! WE'RE HERE! WE'RE HERE!" she screamed. The sky blurred as her eyes filled with tears—the happiest tears of her life.

It was finally time to go home.

READ HOW THE ADVENTURE BEGAN IN

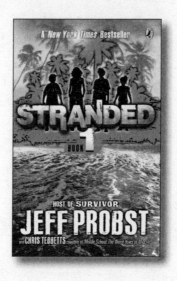

It was supposed to be a vacation—and a chance to get to know one another better. But when a massive storm sets in without warning, four kids are shipwrecked alone on a rocky jungle island in the middle of the South Pacific. No adults. No instructions. Nobody to rely on but themselves. Can they make it home alive?

A week ago, the biggest challenge Vanessa, Buzz, Carter, and Jane had was learning to live as a new blended family. Now the four siblings must find a way to work together if they're going to make it off the island. But first they've got to learn to survive one another.

It was day four at sea, and as far as eleven-year-old Carter Benson was concerned, life didn't get any better than this.

From where he hung, suspended fifty feet over the deck of the *Lucky Star*, all he could see was a planet's worth of blue water. The boat's huge white mainsail ballooned in front of him, filled with a stiff southerly wind that sent them scudding through the South Pacific faster than they'd sailed all week.

This was the best part of the best thing Carter had ever done, no question. It was like sailing and flying at the same time. The harness around his middle held him in place while his arms and legs hung free. The air itself seemed to carry him along, at speed with the boat.

"How you doin' up there, Carter?" Uncle Dexter shouted from the cockpit.

Carter flashed a thumbs-up and pumped his fist. "Faster!" he shouted back. Even with the wind whipping in his ears, Dex's huge belly laugh came back, loud and clear.

Meanwhile, Carter had a job to do. He wound the safety line from his harness in a figure eight around the cleat on the mast to secure himself. Then he reached over and unscrewed the navigation lamp he'd come up here to replace.

As soon as he'd pocketed the old lamp in his rain slicker, he pulled out the new one and fitted it into the fixture, making sure not to let go before he'd tightened it down. Carter had changed plenty of lightbulbs before, but never like this. If anything, it was all too easy and over too fast.

When he was done, he unwound his safety line and gave a hand signal to Dex's first mate, Joe

Kahali, down below. Joe put both hands on the winch at the base of the mast and started cranking Carter back down to the deck.

"Good job, Carter," Joe said, slapping him on the back as he got there. Carter swelled with pride and adrenaline. Normally, replacing the bulb would have been Joe's job, but Dex trusted him to take care of it.

Now Joe jerked a thumb over his shoulder. "Your uncle wants to talk to you," he said.

Carter stepped out of the harness and stowed it in its locker, just like Dex and Joe had trained him to do. Once that was done, he clipped the D-ring on his life jacket to the safety cable that ran the length of the deck and headed toward the back.

It wasn't easy to keep his footing as the *Lucky Star* pitched and rolled over the waves, but even that was part of the fun. If he did fall, the safety cable—also called a jackline—would keep him from going overboard. Everyone was required to stay clipped in when they were on deck, whether they were up there to work . . . or to puke, like Buzz was doing right now.

"Gross! Watch out, Buzz!" Carter said, pushing past him.

"*Uhhhhhnnnnh*" was all Buzz said in return. He was leaning against the rail and looked both green and gray at the same time.

Carter kind of felt sorry for him. They were both eleven years old, but they didn't really have anything else in common. It was like they were having two different vacations out here.

"Gotta keep moving," he said, and continued on toward the back, where Dex was waiting.

"Hey, buddy, it's getting a little choppier than I'd like," Dex said as Carter stepped down into the cockpit. "I need you guys to get below."

"I don't want to go below," Carter said. "Dex, I can help. Let me steer!"

"No way," Dex said. "Not in this wind. You've been great, Carter, but I promised your mom before we set sail—no kids on deck if these swells got over six feet. You see that?" He pointed to the front of the boat, where a cloud of sea spray had just broken over the bow. "*That's* what a six-foot swell looks like. We've got a storm on the way—maybe a big one. It's time for you to take a break."

"Come on, please?" Carter said. "I thought we came out here to sail!"

Dex took him by the shoulders and looked him square in the eye.

"Remember what we talked about before we set out? My boat. My rules. Got it?"

Carter got it, all right. Arguing with Dex was like wrestling a bear. You could try, but you were never going to win.

"Now, grab your brother and get down there," Dex told him.

"Okay, fine," Carter said. "But he's not my brother, by the way. Just because my mom married his dad doesn't mean—"

"Ask me tomorrow if I care," Dexter said, and gave him a friendly but insistent shove. "Now go!"

Benjamin "Buzz" Diaz lifted his head from the rail

and looked out into the distance. All he could see from here was an endless stretch of gray clouds over an endless stretch of choppy waves.

Keeping an eye on the horizon was supposed to help with the seasickness, but so far, all it had done was remind him that he was in the middle of the biggest stretch of nowhere he'd ever seen. His stomach felt like it had been turned upside down and inside out. His legs were like rubber bands, and his head swam with a thick, fuzzy feeling, while the boat rocked and rocked and rocked.

It didn't look like this weather was going to be changing anytime soon, either. At least, not for the better.

Buzz tried to think about something else—anything else—to take his mind off how miserable he felt. He thought about his room back home. He thought about how much he couldn't wait to get there, where he could just close his door and hang out all day if he wanted, playing City of Doom and eating pepperoni pizz—

Wait, Buzz thought. *No. Not that.*

He tried to unthink anything to do with food, but it was too late. Already, he was leaning over the rail again and hurling the last of his breakfast into the ocean.

"Still feeding the fish, huh?" Suddenly, Carter was back. He put a hand on Buzz's arm. "Come on," he said. "Dex told me we have to get below."

Buzz clutched his belly. "Are you kidding?" he said. "Can't it wait?"

"No. Come on."

All week long, Carter had been running around the deck of the *Lucky Star* like he owned it or something. Still, Carter was the least of Buzz's worries right now.

It was only day four at sea, and if things kept going like this, he was going to be lucky to make it to day five.

———

Vanessa Diaz sat at the *Lucky Star*'s navigation station belowdecks and stared at the laptop screen in front of her. She'd only just started to learn about this stuff a few days earlier, but as far as she could tell, all that orange and red on the weather radar was a bad sign. Not to mention the scroll across the bottom of the screen, saying something about "gale-force winds and deteriorating conditions."

The first three days of their trip had been nothing but clear blue skies and warm breezes. Now, nine hundred miles off the coast of Hawaii, all of that had changed. Dexter kept saying they had to adjust their course to outrun the weather, but so far, it seemed like the weather was outrunning them. They'd changed direction at least three times, and things only seemed to be getting worse.

The question was—how *much* worse?

A chill ran down Vanessa's spine as the hatch over the galley stairs opened, and Buzz and Carter came clattering down the steps.

"How are you feeling, Buzzy?" she asked, but he didn't stop to talk. Instead, he went straight for the little bathroom—the "head," Dexter called it—and slammed the door behind him.

Her little brother was getting the worst of these bad seas, by far. Carter, on the other hand, seemed unfazed.

Sometimes Vanessa called them "the twins," as a joke, because they were both eleven but nothing alike. Carter kept his sandy hair cut short and was even kind of muscley for a kid his age. Buzz, on the other hand, had shaggy jet-black curls like their father's and was what adults liked to call husky. The kids at school just called him fat.

Vanessa didn't think her brother was fat—not exactly—but you could definitely tell he spent a lot of time in front of the TV.

"It's starting to rain," Carter said, looking up at the sky.

"Then close the hatch," Vanessa said.

"Don't tell me what to do."

Vanessa rolled her eyes. "Okay, fine. Get wet. See if I care."

He would, too, she thought. He'd just stand there and get rained on, only because she told him not to. Carter was one part bulldog and one part mule.

Jane was there now, too. She'd just come out of the tiny sleeping cabin the two girls shared.

Jane was like the opposite of Carter. She could slip in and out of a room without anyone ever noticing. With Carter, you always knew he was there.

"What are you looking at, Nessa?" Jane asked.

"Nothing." Vanessa flipped the laptop closed. "I was just checking the weather," she said.

There was no reason to scare Jane about all that. She was only nine, and tiny for her age. Vanessa was the oldest, at thirteen, and even though nobody told her to look out for Jane on this trip, she did anyway.

"Dex said there's a storm coming," Carter blurted out. "He said it's going to be major."

"Carter!" Vanessa looked over at him and rolled her eyes in Jane's direction.

But he just shrugged. "What?" he said. "You think she's not going to find out?"

"You don't have to worry about me," Jane said.